INDIGO-35

Nancy Jasin Ensley

Published in the United States of America

ISBN 978-1-970703-46-7 (Paperback)
ISBN 978-1-970703-47-4 (Hardback)
ISBN 978-1-970703-48-1 (eBook)

Library of Congress Control Number: 2026908847

For Book Rights Adaption and other Rights Permission.
Call us at toll-free **601-914-6178**.

TABLE OF CONTENTS

Erin Coutcher entered the glass doors etched with frosted ivy garlands. She took a deep breath in hopes it would calm the butterfly storm rumbling in her stomach. It was her first day in a job she had worked judiciously to obtain. Even as a young girl, Erin had been mesmerized by forensic science. Her brain was wired to dissect everything into its tiniest components. Classmates and family were often exhausted by her questions. "Why?", "How?", "When?", "Because?" was the substance of most of Erin's interactions with others. After graduating from College, Erin searched for the perfect job, one that would challenge her intellect and curiosity. She found the perfect job at SEIS.

Earth has been deteriorating more rapidly over the past twenty years due to inadequate processes to protect air, water, and soil quality. Erin was hired by SEIS, and a few other recently hired scientists were assigned a project to create a semi-permeable substance to block certain chemicals from entering cells. Beneath the rote description of the project lies a secret that will entangle Erin and her project mates in a dangerous mission involving extraterrestrial travel to distant planets, encounters with aliens, and the final days of Earth's deterioration. The metamorphosis of Gerald Porter, CEO of SEIS, from a mild-mannered research scientist to the culmination of the irrational power he holds at this time will challenge those factions who begin to fear his intentions and mental health.

CHAPTER I

UNDETECTED

Nitrogen is an inert gas, meaning it does not react with other gases. It is not toxic in the concentration usually found in our atmosphere. Breathing pure nitrogen is deadly because it displaces oxygen in the lungs. It is odorless, colorless, tasteless, and non-irritating. In other words, it has no properties to warn people of its presence in higher concentrations than the normal of 78%.

There was not much difference between this Wednesday and other Wednesdays in the metropolis of New York City. The early morning traffic danced its staccato rhumba from traffic light to traffic light; trash rode on a stagnant breeze and grabbed hold of the curbs and alleys; crowds of humans shuffled like zombies along the sidewalks. Below the mounds of cement, in tunnels that accommodated murky liquid drainage siphoned from the gutters, rodents ravenously macerated soggy garbage with rabies-infected teeth.

The microscopic, green, translucent particles attached themselves to nitrogen atoms in the polluted air below the surface. The co-opted nitrogen atoms were carried to the manholes and spread undetected into the air.

◄ ◄ ✖ ► ►

Erin Coutcher entered the glass doors etched with frosted ivy garlands. She took a deep breath, hoping to settle the storm of butterflies in her stomach. It was her first day in a job she had worked judiciously to obtain. Even as a young girl Erin had been mesmerized by forensic science. Her mind operated by dissecting everything into its tiniest components. Classmates and family grew weary of her questions. "Why?", "How?", "When?", "Because?" were the substance of most of Erin's interactions with others. Erin's young classmates were content with forgetting most of the lessons the teachers eagerly presented to them. They tolerated the six hours of academia because recess and the few daylight hours after dinner were their reward. Erin did not seem bothered by the cold shoulder she received during her interrogations. If there were a pregnant silence in response to her questions she would go to her room, the library, or a bathroom stall, take out the blue notebook with butterflies geometrically marching across the cover and document her theories, references and queries. The notebook had been a gift from her grandfather, Dr. Joseph R. Coutcher, for her eighth birthday. J.R., as his closest friends were allowed to address him, had come to this country from Germany with his parents when he was three years old. If his parents' status in life had been different, his genius would have been recognized in childhood. German immigrants who relocated to the United States after WWII were generally unwelcome.

2

J.R.'s parents worked two jobs in order to afford the rent for their tiny, two-bedroom apartment and put food on the table. J.R. swept floors in businesses near his apartment and rode his dilapidated bicycle through the neighborhood delivering newspapers. He placed one dime from his earnings into a Mason jar he hid under his bed. The rest of his pay was given to his father and mother. His curiosity sometimes led to experiments with insects, cleaning product concoctions, recipes with noxious aromas and burned utensils. After years of hard work and intense study J.R. from the projects became Dr. Joseph R. Coutcher, Surgeon General of the United States of America for three Presidential terms. His resume' included several textbooks on epidemiology, ecology and astrophysics. He invented devices and equipment to decrease pollution in industry. His discoveries in the transmission and treatment of communicable disease were utilized world-wide. Erin inherited her grandfather's genius and passion for exploration and epidemiology. She received her master's degree in epidemiology and a PhD in astrophysics.

The Stockton Institute of Epidemiological Study (SIES) was located on the ninth floor of the Tremont Tower Plaza, three blocks East of Times Square in New York City. Erin ran her hands over her navy-blue skirt before she pushed the elevator button for the ninth floor. Erin had not been blessed with the height she identified with prestige, nor the manageable shiny straight hair of the businesswomen and scientists pictured on the covers of medical and political magazines. She stood erect with her shoulders back and her chest out in a military pose to enhance her five-foot-two-inch frame. She wrestled her frizzy auburn hair into a bun, secured with a small army of hairpins and a barrette. She perched non-prescription dark-rimmed glasses on the end of her pug nose hoping to make her nose appear more aquiline. Erin had the ability to memorize multiple formulas, identify organisms and their pathology from memory and dissect mathematic problems into solvable categories, but had difficulty choosing which one of her two suits to wear on her first day as Research Coordinator at SIES. She glanced demurely at the two men in identical dark blue suits with dazzling white shirts and matching blue and yellow striped ties. Both men were about six feet tall and had salt and pepper grey hair. They stared straight ahead when Erin entered the elevator. She noticed there were no other floor buttons pushed so she asked them "what floor?" after she pushed the button for the ninth floor. Neither blinked nor answered. It did not seem to Erin that they noticed she had boarded the elevator. She was too anxious to care about them. She assumed they wanted the same destination. The three passengers exited the elevator on the ninth floor. Erin watched the two strange men walk rigidly down the hall and enter an office or hallway several feet from the elevator. Erin shook her head and approached the reception desk.

"Could you please direct me to the research department? My name is—

"Erin Coutcher." The perfectly coiffed receptionist completed Erin's sentence. The badge read KAREN TURNER, RECEPTIONIST SIES - 99. "Ms. Coutcher turn left at the hallway just past the office marked *Private*. Use the code on this card to access the double doors marked *Research Portal*. You will follow the directions once you enter." The receptionist handed Erin a plastic card with SIES-111 stamped on it.

"Thank you, Ms. Turner," Erin smiled. Ms. Turner had returned to her computer, ignoring Erin.

At the edge of another universe, light years away from Earth, orbiting along the very edge of its Goldilocks's Zone, a planet comparable in size to Earth and orbiting at a similar distance from its twin suns was beginning to surround itself with a protective radiation-like layer.

 0-10

Vincent D'Amato prided himself on owning the finest Italian restaurant in Manhattan. The five-star rating, earned through his management skills and culinary expertise in original Italian dishes also advertised personal attention to a cadre of prominent politicians, businessmen and millionaires. D'Amato's had grown from a small carry-out to an elegant dining experience offering a gourmet menu prepared by famous chefs and presented by courteous and professional staff. Specialties included:

Lasagna Bolognaise

Fritto Misto di Mare

Eggplant in Picante

Sausage and Broccoli Frittata

Vincent complimented the ambience with his Mediterranean charm and handsome face. Deep set hazel eyes with flecks of gold, thick charcoal black hair and olive skin accented his Romanesque nose and high cheek bones. He worked out in the spacious and professionally equipped gym in his stately mansion on the outskirts of the city. The resulting physique filled out his expensive suits. The cologne *Fierce Intense* was delicate and masculine, causing the female patrons to swoon as he leaned near them at a respectful distance.

Wednesdays were usually one of the restaurant's busiest days, especially during the evening. Preferential reservations for prestigious patrons were taken from six o'clock pm until nine o'clock pm the first and third Wednesdays of each month. Victor scheduled the most eye pleasing and specially trained staff for those evenings. He moved gracefully among the linen covered tables, greeting his influential guests.

"Buona sera, Signor, Signora, Signorina." Shards of light from the candles nestled in cut crystal vases darted in triangular patterns across the tablecloths. Wilson Eddleman and Richard Quincy chose one of the booths in a secluded corner of the restaurant. They swirled the golden toothpick with an onion-filled olive in the martinis in front of them. Senator Wilson Eddleman was sixty-four years old. He had been attracted to politics from his first elected position as President of his high school senior class. After college he served as Mayor of St. Louis, Governor of Missouri, and finally winning a Senatorial seat sixteen years ago. He never lost a race, and he did not intend to lose this one.

Richard Quincy scanned the menu and the room. His dark green eyes appeared cat-like with thick brown eyebrows connected in the middle of his furrowed brow. He always seemed to be scowling even when the rest of his face was laughing. He was short in stature, barely reaching five feet, eight inches. His muscular physique made up for the lack of height. The long chestnut hair was pulled back into a neat ponytail. The beginnings of a beard shadowed his jaw just enough to make him look somewhat sinister.

Wilson broke the silence. "I need an update, Quincy." He whispered, his lips barely moving.

"You need to be patient, Will." Richard smiled flashing his pearly white teeth with one gold incisor in the bottom front. The waitress was beautiful but not flashy. Victor personally interviewed all the staff he hired, choosing a few special ones to grace his Wednesdays. All his waitresses and waiters were attractive, educated and well spoken. He stressed that they were not to highlight their sexuality as they needed to please both the male and female patrons, especially not posing a threat to the opposite sex in the party. Angelina stood the appropriate distance from the table.

"Buona sera, gentlemen. May I take your order?" Would you like me to repeat our specials of the evening?" Both men ordered. When Angelina brought the delicacies to the table, neither Wilson nor Richard noticed the tiny microphone and recorder glued to the underside of their dinner plates.

The green particles grabbed hold of the nitrogen atoms. Tentacles sprouted from the particles' cell body and began a slow integration of R-125 DNA modification.

◄ ◄ ✗ ► ►

Erin opened the thick steel door with one small blue-tinted window which led her into a small anteroom. The door closed and locked behind her.

A deep male voice echoed against the tile walls of the room. "Dr. Coutcher, please place all jewelry, phones, and personal items in the cabinet marked with your identification. Lock the cabinet and place the wrist band with the key attached on your right wrist." Erin tried to see if there were cameras or microphones anywhere in the room. None were visible, so she complied.

"Put on the coveralls, mask, shoe, head covers and goggles in the packet on the shelf marked with your identification." Erin donned the protective gear.

"Push the red button next to the elevator and enter. Erin watched as one of the walls parted revealing an elevator. She entered cautiously. Her heart rate increased as the elevator sped upward. In less than thirty seconds the door opened, and the voice continued. "Exit the elevator." The room was pure white and brightly lit, the lights coming from the walls, ceiling and even the floor. Against the wall cubicles covered with transparent shells housed people dressed the same as Erin. The cubicles were filled with banks of computers, cupboards, laboratory equipment and a curved desk. Centrifuges and racks of test tubes lined the counters of the desks.

"Dr. Coutcher, your Captain will be with you to begin your orientation." From a huge eggshell shaped structure at the back side of the room a man who looked like her stiff companions on the elevator walked toward her. The man seemed to have walked through the wall of the structure as if it were invisible.

"Dr. Coutcher, welcome to SIES. My name is 0-10. I will be your Captain during the orientation period." 0-10's eyes seemed to look through her and yet focus on her simultaneously.

Erin had been hired for the position through an on-line advertisement. There was a virtual interview with a faceless person after her resume' was chosen as a possible candidate. She received instructions on her computer to report to the ninth-floor reception desk at the Tremont Tower Plaza on Wednesday, October 14, 2012, at 8:00 am. She had been working on her thesis for a doctorate in Environmental and Epidemiological Research. She danced around her apartment, called her family and a few friends to share the news. The rest of the instructions were brief.

You will be directed to the Epidemiological Laboratory, assigned a Captain who will guide you through the six-week orientation process. Pending the results of the evaluation of your orientation period you will be considered for the full-time position of Coordinator of Project Indigo-35. Should you fail to pass the benchmark of expertise and security required for this position, you will be relieved of your duties.

No personal items, cellular phones or jewelry will be allowed in the Laboratory.

Welcome to the esteemed SIES family,

Dr. Gerald Proctor

President, CEO

0-10 motioned to Erin to follow him. He led her to an unoccupied cubicle marked with a name plate.

DR. ERIN COUTCHER, EPIDEMIOLOGICAL TECHNICIAN
SIES # 111; Indigo-35F

0-10 opened drawers and cabinets allowing Erin time to inspect the contents. She was amazed at the caliber and the completeness of the items she would need to perform tests and measurements. Test tubes, racks, pipettes, chemicals in clearly marked containers, face shields, and other tools of the trade were skillfully placed in labeled drawers and slots. "Please take the next thirty minutes to look through your station. Document any equipment or supplies you might need that are not included here, the reason for your request and the amount needed." 0-10 handed her a dry erase board with a marker attached. Erin noted there were no pens, pencils or scratch paper in the cubicle cabinets or drawers. The usual desk carrier, stocked with assorted scissors, tape, markers, paper clips was also absent.

Maybe I have to get that stuff myself. Erin thought.

"You will not be supplying any items from outside this room." 0-10 stated to Erin's surprise.

"Gosh, he's reading my thoughts. How is that possible?"

"Some rules may seem odd at first. You will become accustomed to them," 0-10 said without changing his expression.

"Still creepy." Erin thought. Her buddy, 0-10, spent the next two hours training Erin on the computer system. All notes were to be documented in the "notes" section of the system. Each week technicians were assigned a new password. Any documentation deleted would remain

on the mainframe. No e-mails could be sent to persons or places outside of those authorized by SIES. A list of personnel with whom Erin could correspond appeared on the "contacts" file. All documentation would be backed up to the mainframe after 5:30 pm daily. Computers automatically shut down at 5:25 pm each day. All internet queries (Google, WebMD, etc.) would be monitored and filtered by SIES. Social Media sites (Facebook, LinkedIn, Instagram, etc.) were not available to technicians. Erin was directed to contact her Captain if there are any problems or questions. Erin had written PHONE, PAGER, PAD AND PENCILS FOR DOODLING on the dry erase board.

"You may have one pencil and three sheets of blank paper. All doodles and written notes will be placed in the slot to your right by the end of each shift. Phones are not provided. I will be available when you press the red button next to your computer. You will have no need of a phone in the Laboratory." 0-10 answered in his monotone voice.

"Holy crap! This is ...." Erin stopped her thoughts since 0-10 would probably report her if she got feisty. By noon 0-10 had shown Erin the project she would be working on. Instructions, formulas, and directions to sites needed to access information pertaining to Indigo-35, the project assigned to her team, were listed on a daily computerized worksheet.

In lay terms, the portion of the indigo project that was Erin's team responsibility was to find a substance to coat healthy cells. This semi-permeable armor would be programmed to block certain substances, such as pesticides, from entering the cell while allowing healthy substances, such as nutrients, to pass through. There were eighteen technicians, some of them were coordinators assigned to other team projects in the lab. Each technician was privy to information related only to the assigned project or portion of a project. Erin was introduced to the three technicians with whom she would be working.

Henry Stutkowski – Indigo-35G; Madeline Weber – Indigo-35H; Martin Szechnick – Indigo-35I. All three had impressive credentials similar to Erin's. 0-10 did not introduce any of the other teams to her, nor had the members of Erin's team been introduced to or corresponded with the other teams. In other words, stay in your own lane. Erin had to test the thought transmission mystery. She closed her eyes and thought, *Maybe I can talk to one of the other project leaders to see what they are working on.* 0-10 put his hand on Erin's shoulder. She felt a jolt of electricity, followed by an icy sensation spreading down her arm.

"This project is top secret, and teams are not allowed to discuss any part of their portion with other teams or leaders, Dr. Coutcher." 0-10 released his hand from Erin's shoulder and the icy, electric feeling gradually left. Erin shivered and nodded to 0-10 that she understood.

CHAPTER III

LIGHT YEARS

A light year is the distance light travels in one year. One light year is about 5.88 trillion miles, 9.5 trillion Km. Humans cannot reach the speed of light because they have mass. Baryonic matter consists of subatomic particles such as protons and neutrons. "Dark matter" is non-baryonic, devoid of protons and neutrons. When traveling in space the faster a ship goes the more energy has to be exerted to increase the speed. In order to accelerate to such speeds, one would have to increase the speed of the universe surrounding the ship. In order to approach the speed of light a bubble around the ship would need to totally separate it from the rest of the universe. The space between the bubble and the ship would then become the ship's universe. The ship could accelerate by binding with the space within that bubble. To race into the future would require incredible amounts of energy— the energy equivalent needed to control space in front of the bubble and expand space behind that bubble. This would require an engine and a ship manufactured from exotic matter. The Earth is hundreds of years from developing such a model. *

Light travels at 186,000 miles per second. If a ship traveled at 99.5% of the speed of light. Leaving on December 25, 2012, for five years traveling at the speed of light, the crew would have aged five years, but everyone on Earth would have aged twenty-five years. It would be 2037 when the ship returned. The negative (exotic) mass would possess strange properties. It would be able to accelerate in the direction opposite to the applied force. It would construct artificial worm holes.

Some German scientists launched a tiny atom-packed ship into space and blasted it with lasers. They created the first exotic state of matter known as the Bone-Einstein Condensate (BEC) in space. When a cloud of atoms is exposed to extreme cold (absolute 0), minus 459.67 degrees F, they stop acting like individual atom. They clump together but occupy the lowest possible energy state. The clump of atoms looks no different than the single atom.

The BEC in space could boost the hunt for gravitational atoms so that a manned spaceship, enclosed in its own universe could travel at the speed of light. Indigo-35 was the name given to the planet that had been discovered one year prior to Erin's entrance into the SIES world. The planet is forty-three light years from earth, orbiting the same distance from its sun as earth. There was a possibility of the planet having water on or below its surface which would give it the ability to support life forms or have some form of life already existing there.

Senator Eddleman and Richard Query ate their meals in silence. Both men had been thrown into a conundrum that neither fully understood. Wilson had climbed the political ladder from law school to City Counsel, to Mayor, to Governor, to the U.S. Senate. During that pursuit Wilson and Richard had lost touch with one another. One week after Wilson was re-elected to the Senate for the fourth term, he received an unusual phone call. His secretary filtered all of the Senator's calls. She had been working for him for over twenty years learning everything from his thoughts on high profile issues to what kind of toothpaste he used.

"Hello, Ms. Beckman," the caller stated her name before she could answer with her usual "Good morning, Senator Eddleman's office, Esther Beckman speaking."

"Please state your ID code or full name, title and the reason for your call." Esther answered so many calls a day she could multitask as well as perform her telephone duties. She continued to do some work on her computer.

"Ms. Beckman, please tell the Senator Dr. Gerald Proctor wishes to speak to him, Code 2339." Esther could not recall hearing that name in the past. She wanted to ask the person with a deep, gravelly voice how he knew her name. She elected not to ask. She asked him to hold while she searched her computer for Code 2339. The picture of a distinguished man with silver hair and a handsome face appeared on the screen.

Gerald Samuel Proctor, MS, PhD, FACS
BD August 11, 01/21/1947; Code 2339
President SIES, Department of Epidemiology/Universal
Science and Exploration

Fingerprints, current and past addresses, phone numbers, background check results, personal history, education, past positions held, job history, etc. could also be accessed from the secure site. Esther asked the caller to state the reason for the call.

"The Senator may not remember me from his college days. I have a project I wish to present to him." Gerald answered. Esther asked the caller to excuse her while she contacted Wilson on the intercom. Wilson was puzzled but took the call out of curiosity. He knew of SIES. He had not had any dealings with the company nor this Dr. Proctor. He tried to remember friends from college. The name Gerald Proctor did not sound familiar. Esther had forwarded his information and his picture, but he could not place him. He picked up the phone. "Dr. Proctor, this is Senator Eddleman. How can I help you?"

"You may not remember me, Senator. I was your lab partner in advanced chemistry class at Berkeley. I was the geeky guy with a bowl haircut, my mother's rendition, and horn-rimmed glasses." Wilson still could not remember him.

"Good to hear from you, Gerald, after all these years. Advanced Chemistry was a tough class." Wilson said with as much enthusiasm as he could pretend.

"I'm not a very memorable person. I pretty much kept to myself. Even now, I prefer to be alone, though my position requires otherwise." the caller offered. "You may be familiar with the Stockton Institute of Epidemiological Study, SIES. I am President of the company, and we are working on a project to create a protective covering for living cells. This covering would keep out damaging chemicals and organisms while allowing vital nutrients and chemicals into the cells in space. The Universe as we know it is in the Dark Energy Age; the sixth and final era. Large scale structures in our universe are ceasing to grow. Structures that are bound by gravity will remain bound once dark energy takes over. Those that are not already bound will accelerate away from one another. Galaxies and clusters of galaxies will merge into one large elliptical galaxy. I would like the opportunity to explain this further, as you can see this is complicated."

"Dr. Proctor, I am not sure what part I would play in that sort of project."

"If you would have about one hour in the next two weeks to meet with me, I could explain it to you. Could you please look at your calendar and see if that is possible? I will be happy to meet at a location that is convenient for you. It should be somewhere where we can speak privately." Wilson could hear the urgency in Dr. Proctor's voice.

"Gerald, I will have my secretary, Esther, schedule an hour sometime this week. We can meet here in my office. Otherwise, you would have to tolerate the entourage of Secret Service men that follow me everywhere."

"Thank you, Sir, for agreeing to meet with me." They both hung up. Wilson still could not remember Gerald Proctor, but that was a long time ago.

As the Dark Energy era progresses, radiation will eject stars into the abyss and planets will spiral into parent stars. Black holes will decay. This is projected to occur in thousands of years if the trajectory remains predictable. Any untoward changes in the Universe could escalate the process. A Black Hole is a place in space where gravity pulls so much that even light cannot get out. The reason gravity is so strong is that matter is squeezed into a tiny space.

During the six-week orientation period Erin met with her team members several times under the close scrutiny of 0-10. The team members had found a way to disguise their thoughts that 0-10 did not seem to notice. If they sang a tune in their minds or even hummed it out loud, the thoughts and questions they had were not recognized. Each of them would write on the dry erase board in a code they had invented, to set up a get together after work hours at one of their homes. They were careful to erase the coded message as soon as it was seen by the members. They surmised that something in their protective goggles accessed a part of their brains to transmit their thoughts, so they removed the goggles before they entered the changing space. 0-10 was most certainly some type of a robot. Glancing around the room at the other cubicles, other Captains in the area looked the same and acted the same as their 0-10. Erin was impressed with the progress her teammates had made in testing several prototypes despite the restraints SIES placed on them. After the six weeks orientation was completed and was deemed acceptable, Erin's title was upgraded to Coordinator.

Senator Eddleman met with Dr. Proctor several days after the first phone call. Dr. Proctor was asking Wilson to draft a Bill for five point two million dollars to fund an exploration in space to evaluate levels of radiation and to test materials that could possibly be used to protect a spacecraft with a probe on board to send pictures of Mars back to earth. The real goal of the project could not be released. Gerald and several other scientists planned to attempt a trip beyond Mars to planets light years away. It would take many years to access the information. NASA agreed with SEIS that starting as soon as possible would be advantageous. Such legislation would be a difficult endeavor to even get through committee let alone get a bill to the floor of both Houses. Funding a project that was based on projections way into the future with no immediate benefits would be almost impossible. Wilson saw the urgency in Gerald's face. He put together a proposal for funding and sent it to the Department of Interior, the Secretary of Defense and the President's top security advisor. He also took advantage of his relationships with powerful, rich, and philanthropic people he had met and worked with throughout the years. Richard Quincy was one of them. Gerald stressed the actual reason for the project be kept top secret. If the general public got wind of a spacecraft probing a distant planet it might cause public panic. He could see the headlines, *End of world predicted.* Scientists sending spaceships to other planets to look for a way to save the human race!" When Wilson approached Richard about investing millions of dollars to send a spacecraft into the Universe to collect data on radiation levels, Richard seemed interested. He always had a fascination with space travel and the science of creation. The sum of money requested would not make a dent in his wealth. He was enough of a narcissist to envision his name on the side of the spacecraft. What Gerald did not reveal to either investor was how great the urgency was. The scientists had estimated the Earth could be catastrophically disrupted in 150 years. If life could exist on a planet different from the gravitational changes presently occurring in the Earths orbital path, mega spacecrafts could be built with a protective capsule around them so as to encompass their own universe. Specially chosen men and women could man the spacecraft and be transported through time and space to the distant planet. Unaware of the true purpose, certain SIES technicians were charged with inventing a semipermeable substance with nitrogen as its prime ingredient believing their work was to block chemicals in pesticides and other toxic chemicals from entering plant cells, they would not know the true reason for their research. Gerald and a handful of his most trusted cohorts were the few who knew they were close to a solution to create the bubble for the spacecraft. Perhaps actual exotic matter was close to being discovered.

During Henry's experiments he was puzzled by barely undetectable increases in atmospheric nitrogen. It had been proven that carbon dioxide levels increased due to greenhouse gas effects. The inert quality of nitrogen (odorless, tasteless, non-combustible) and its availability in exhaled air (78%) made it an ideal chemical to use in creating the cell coating membrane. He had not pursued investigation of the increase as it most likely was the result of global warming. The World Health Organization (WHO) noticed a very slight increase in reported cases of dementia, seizures, developmental delays, and deaths. They felt these statistics were being reported more efficiently thus causing a rise in collected data. Henry was a graduate of MIT with a Master's in astrophysics and a PhD in computer science. He worked with John McCarthy who was the founder of Artificial Intelligence. In 1955 Herbert A. Simon, Turing, Minsk, and Newell developed logic programming language used to create more logically equivalent programs. AI simulates the information processing of human consciousness and thinking. Strong AI machines are capable of experiencing consciousness. Henry was the least conversant of the team members. Most of the time he communicated electronically and in one-word responses. "Hmm," "Perhaps," "Yes," "No," and "Ahem" were about as close to verbal communication as he dared.

Madeline seemed relieved to have another woman on the team. All the rest of the technicians appeared to be men though it was difficult to tell when everyone looked alike dressed in their coveralls, goggles and masks. Not that Madeline Weber PhD was ever intimidated by a man. She usually was the one that intimidated her colleagues. Abandoned by her birth mother when she was almost three years old, she spent most of the next fourteen years in different foster homes. She learned to fight her own battles, and after excelling in high school, she received several scholarships for college. Southern California University was where she graduated at the top of her class and went on the receive her PhD in chemical engineering and epidemiology. Madeline had a rigid posture - all five feet-eleven inches of her. Her trim, athletic build added to her air of confidence. Coal-black hair, worn in a pageboy, framed her pale face. Deep blue eyes draped in long black lashes seemed to bore into anyone who she was addressing. She rarely blinked, which also caused people to be uncomfortable around her.

Martin Szechnick functioned as the mediator in the intellectual battles between Henry and Madeline. Henry and Madeline were a dysfunctional yin and yang. Just when there appeared to be a mesh between their theories one or the other would rip them apart. Martin was an expert in atmospheric and high-altitude research. He had worked at NASA for fourteen years in that program. He also had a passion for the improvement of AI, professing that "robotic humans" were a possibility. Martin was average in height and average build with a pleasant "average" looking face. That was all that was average about him. He was a genius. All three of Erin's teammates had been working at SIES for almost a year. They had successfully completed several assignments when they were given the Indigo-35 project two months before Erin was hired. Madeline and Henry were at odds about a formula for a substance to be tested by bombarding cells with a radioactive nitrogen/lithium laser to produce membrane separation. These membranes act as a selective barrier allowing relatively free passage of one component while restraining another. Based on an existing application, the removal of dissolved oxygen from water in the preparation of power plant boiler feed water was already being performed. On a large scale this same application can be obtained by running water and nitrogen countercurrent to each other in a packed tower. Henry and Madeline tested a substance created by exposing nitrogen/lithium atoms to -0 temperatures. The atoms were permeable to all nutrients and chemicals needed for cell growth, but a rare chemical found in pesticides and other caustic substances, Chlorpyrifos, still managed to pass through the membrane.

Martin theorized exposure to near-absolute zero (-495°F) caused atomic clumping and changed the gravitational pull in order to force the undesirable chemical away from the cell wall. Erin added another factor to the equation. If Martin's theory were to prove successful, could that principle be applied to other genres? Perhaps it could be used in industry, health care, even the space program.

0-10 had lessened his observation visits after Erin graduated from her orientation and was given the title of Coordinator. After the team meeting where Erin discussed this principle with the three teammates, 0-10 morphed through the transparent-appearing membrane and walked into her cubicle. He was the only "person" who could enter a cubicle without the teammates' permission.

"Team Indigo-35 will focus on the creation of a substance to coat cells blocking pesticides from entering. No other uses will be researched after that is accomplished." 0-10's voice always gave Erin a chill. Erin acknowledged his directive. She and her teammates had discovered humming tunes or visualizing they were playing in an orchestra, blocked thoughts that they did not want 0-10 or anyone else to be able to access. When technicians and coordinators left work, it seemed that "mind reading" did not occur outside of SIES. The members of the team all felt it had to do with something hidden in the work apparel and equipment they were ordered to wear in the lab. Somehow one of them would have to smuggle a pack containing those items out of the lab.

It was 5:25 pm on Wednesday, three months after Erin became coordinator of her team. Erin had observed the routine visits of 0-10 and the other captains. There had been no new technicians brought in for orientation in the past few months. 0-10 visited Team I-35 every three weeks for thirty minutes as was routine for the other captains. Each cubicle or pod was composed of four members, one of which was a coordinator. There were a total of eighteen pods, including I-35. There were four captains, all dressed the same with the same unexpressive face and demeanor. Each captain was overseeing six to seven pods. According to Erin's calculation there were only two opportunities when all captains were not moving about the pods. One was at 4:00 pm-5:30 pm. At 5:30 pm the captains made rounds to confirm employees were exiting and de-frocking in their respective anterooms. They also confirmed that the 5:25 pm daily back-up of computers had been completed. The second opportunity was when lunch breaks were rotated, four pods at a time. Lunches were prepared and organized by SIES, served in the giant lunchroom, located to the right of the large egg-shaped structure from which the captains entered and exited. The lunchroom was circular. The lighting in the walls and ceiling mimicked sunlight. Soft music mixed with birds' chirping sounds, fresh air filtering throughout the structure and a dome portraying videos of relaxing scenes from all over the world added to the ambiance. The atmosphere of the lunchroom made one feel they were sitting outside on a sunny day. Colorful cushioned couches and chairs with trays attached to accommodate the healthy lunches and smoothies provided by SIES completed a relaxing atmosphere. Each pod was enclosed in an invisible shield that allowed the visible amenities in but none of the conversation or visibility of members in the pod out for other pod members to see. The time allotted for the lunch period included one of the two-bathroom breaks per day. Smoking was prohibited throughout the entire building. A second bathroom break per person could be taken with permission from the captain. Video monitors were installed in the lunchroom and the bathrooms. The only privacy was in the bathroom stalls. Men's urinals were located in the bathroom stalls as well as a toilet. If additional breaks were needed due to female problems or leaky bowels, the employee was sent home for the rest of the day. Sick days could be taken as long as the employee called in at least one hour before his or her workday began. Emergencies were only excused if a physician notified the pod's captain. Three hours were scheduled for the entire workforce lunch breaks. Sixteen employees with thirty-minute lunches and breaks, ten minutes between each session for cleanup, moved efficiently between 11:00 am and 2:00 pm. I-35 team's lunch period was scheduled from 1:30 pm to 2:00 pm. From 12:00 pm to 1:00 pm the captains were focused on keeping things flowing seamlessly. Their attention was diverted away from the pods awaiting their turns or those that had already had their lunch break.

0-10 did not notice Madeline slither toward the anteroom that serviced the least number of technicians on that Wednesday. Pods Twelve and Thirteen were each short one technician, both out with an unspecified ailment. Madeline could see there were fewer people in both pods. 0-10 had asked all the team members if they had experienced headaches, confusion, and nausea that morning. I-35H was symptom free. Madeline's technical ingenuity was useful outside the assigned projects. She had requested a walk around the periphery of the lab two times a day because of her back pain when sitting too long. This was a documented problem listed in her health history resulting from an automobile accident several years ago. 0-10 gave permission for the ten-minute walks two times a day. While passing the pods she ran her keycard past each of the magnetic pads that were programmed differently for each pod team. In the few seconds as she passed her card under the lower portion of the magnetic pad, green lights flashed the four-code sequence so rapidly that it would be impossible for anyone to commit them to memory—anyone except Madeline. Her photographic memory imprinted the codes for all the pods in her exceptional brain, including the access codes for Pods Twelve and Thirteen. During the minimally monitored time by the captains at lunch period Madeline stealthily opened pod thirteen, interrupted the sensor that would alarm and turn on the lights with a magnet device she had smuggled in the lining of her brassiere. In the darkness she took the elevator to Pod thirteen's dressing room, de-magnetized the lights and alarm grabbed one of the packets containing the protective supplies and slipped it under her coverall. She cinched the packet with the belt around her waist that was part of her coverall and moved cautiously back into the elevator and up to the lab proper. She walked with a slight limp back to I-35H pod (just for effect) and proceeded to act involved with the image on the computer screen.

CHAPTER IV

SECRETS

Wilson and Richard were awaiting an update on the progress of the Indigo project. The Bill for funding had squeaked through the Appropriations Committee and was scheduled to go to the House floor in a week. The Senator needed information to validate the importance of the project as well as its potential to highlight the present administration's goal of enhancing the space program.

Gerald Proctor, CEO of SIES, had spent a good portion of his forty years as a scientist working on research projects in Pharmaceutical and Industrial companies. He had a comfortable life, a wife and two children who were grown and successful in their chosen professions. He wasn't sure if on his fifty-eighth birthday he had a stroke, a mid-life crisis or just got plain bored with the monotony of his job. He went to work at Ascot Pharmaceuticals, Inc. with his usual lunch efficiently placed in a brown paper bag: bologna and cheese with mustard, an apple, and a small box of raisins for his immune system. He punched in at his usual 7:30 am, thirty minutes before his shift began, and walked into his laboratory cubicle to set up the usual chemicals, flasks and test tubes. On his chair there was a book. He looked around the lab, but no one was in yet, as usual. The title of the book was *Apathy Be Damned.* Gerald wasn't used to anything upsetting his routine. He came in early so that he could review his research and set up in the peace and quiet before the other technicians arrived. He picked up the book and looked at the picture of the author. In the black and white photograph, a handsome, middle-aged man with salt and pepper greying hair, dressed in a sweater seemed to be looking right at him. The man was smiling. He looked content and confident. Gerald read the synopsis on the back cover.

Have you become so apathetic that you never take risks, dream, or change your routine? Is every day a rubber stamp of the day before? Are you too comfortable, bored, restless? I challenge you to read this book and I guarantee it will change your life. Take this chance to unlock a part of you that will give you the courage to blaze a new trail.

All through the day that paragraph kept seeping into Gerald's concentration. That evening he took the book home. He kissed his wife, Emily, ate his dinner and complimented her on her cooking (as he had done for all twenty-seven years of their marriage). He read the paper, really just gazed at it, the pages blurred as the words of the author of the book echoed within him. He threw a tattered toy around the living room for Duke, their drooling Labrador, as he had done every night, then took him for a short walk. He showered and went to bed at the usual time, 9:00 pm sharp, hugged Emily and tried to sleep. By 1:00 am he had only pretended to sleep. He inched out of bed and tiptoed downstairs to his study. Sitting in his Lazy-Boy he read the entire book. By the morning, he was no longer "usual" Gerald Proctor. He arrived at work at 8:00 am, not his usual 7:30 start.

People looked at him as though he was a new employee punching in with the rest of the crew. Instead of going to his cubicle he knocked on his supervisor's office door. When he was asked to come in, he handed an envelope to the man who barely knew him.

"I want to thank you for trusting me with all the projects I have completed these past eight years and for the experience I have gained while with this company. Please accept my resignation and make arrangements to release my 401-K." Mr. Below, the supervisor, looked up. His brow crinkled as he tried to remember the man standing on the other side of his desk.

"Pardon me? I'm sorry I don't remember you. You work in this department?" Mr. Below asked.

"Yes, sir. I have worked in the research laboratory for eight years." Gerald Proctor…. Sir." Gerald stood as tall as he could with a confident look on his face.

"Oh, yes, Proctor. You are resigning? Are you giving your two-week notice?"

"No, sir, I have an opportunity that required I start work this Monday. I can only give you these next four days."

"Your position requires you to give at least a two-week notice." Mr. Below said in his usual dictatorial voice.

"I am sorry, sir. I will leave detailed instructions and information on the progress of the present project for my successor."

"Your severance will be much less if you leave by the end of the week."

"As long as I can access the funds in my retirement, I will have to be satisfied with the severance allowed." The "old" Gerald would have wilted by now, but this wasn't the "old" Gerald.

Mr. Below was paying more attention now. "You will not take any of the information about projects with you when you leave. I accept your resignation. Can I ask you if you have a reason for leaving other than this so-called opportunity?"

"Apathy, sir. Just plain apathy." With that, he turned and quietly left Mr. Below's office and went to his cubicle.

Beneath Gerald Proctor's calm, non-confrontational exterior there smoldered a driven, risk hungry genius. The Jekyll and Hyde, the Ying and Yang or just the Mid-life Crisis syndrome erupted. He was going to make his mark in this world. When he arrived home that evening, he kissed Emily more passionately than he had in years, told her to sit down and revealed he had quit his job. Emily looked at the man standing in front of her who was not the predictable, softspoken husband she knew. This Gerald seemed taller, more energized, and confident. Even his voice was deeper and commanding. He took her hands in his. "Emily, I know this is a shock. I've always lived my life in a mold I thought I needed to be safe. I have so many dreams and ideas I have never had the courage to test. There is a research institute in New York that was looking for someone with my qualifications to head their research department. I interviewed for the position, and they want me to start next Monday. I am so excited."

Emily didn't know what to say. "New York? We would have to sell this house and move. I'm happy for you, dear, but this is so sudden."

"I know, honey. We can put the house up for sale. I have already contacted a realtor and she feels it would be snatched up in no time." Gerald watched as Emily stared at him, her face turning pale and tears welling up in her eyes. "Oh, Ems, don't cry. It isn't that far from Summit—the kids will be closer. We can get a nice apartment; we don't need this big house with all this land." Gerald pulled her to him and held her tightly.

"My garden…our church…. our friends." She sobbed, her tears leaving a wet spot on his shirt.

Gerald held her away from him. "Ems, I need to do this. I can't live another day feeling like I am a robot, never taking any risks. I am going to do this. You can stay here until the house is sold. I can look for an apartment while I am being oriented to the job. You can come on the week-ends until the house is sold." Emily looked into the eyes of the man she loved with all her heart. This was someone she did not know at all. She turned and walked, her legs feeling like rubber, up the stairs to their bedroom. After several minutes she heard tapping at the door.

"Ems, can I come in. Let's talk about this."

"Go away, Gerry. I don't know you right now." She laid down on the fluffy comforter and cried into her fluffy pillow. Six months later Emily moved into the posh apartment on the tenth floor of a building that overlooked Central Park. The apartment was tastefully decorated and furnished by a famous interior decorator. Gerald had impressed the Board of Directors in just the few months he was on the job that he was already in line for a vice-presidential position. The prestigious company had accolades from many scientific genres. There were four main research branches in various large cities across the United States. The New York branch focused on chemical substance transport development and astrophysics. As Gerald Proctor gained status and recognition, he became obsessed with finding a planet in the Universe that could support life. Though there had been many theories on how to accomplish space travel at the speed of light, none had been successful.

Indigo-35 was a planet that appeared to be slightly larger than Earth. This calculation was made using measurements of radiological beams emitted from asteroids hitting the planet's surface. No real visualization was possible that many light years in space. The size, distance from the sun and other properties were extrapolated from data based on radiation from the bombardment of particles in space that traveled through the Universe unaltered. Below the surface of Indigo-35 there were zones constructed of materials not yet known to Earth's human race. Artificial Intelligence here was thousands of years ahead of Earth's technology. The Indigo occupants were able to think, move and live the same as their early human counterparts. Somewhere in the development, the humans were overtaken by their own inventions. Devoid of emotion, the Apellonauts, as they had been christened during their early development, overtook their human inventors, destroyed them and multiplied via a strange form of osmosis into a population of robotic, blue-tinged beings with six arms, each expanding into twelve digits, a pedicle extending from the enormous oblong head to the lower end of the creature could change its mobility tail into wheels, jets, air compressors, weapons; whatever the terrain or confrontation dictated. Large opaque eyes stood several inches on a stem at the upper part of the head. The stem could rotate the eyes 360 degrees. An Apellonaut could see in any direction. In each eye tiny crystal strands sent information to the mainframe located at the back of the head. The mainframe was encased in an impenetrable substance that was not known to Earthlings. Communication was accomplished digitally through sensors in the "fingers" at end of the arms. These digits gave off cyber signals transmitted from the mainframe or "brain" of the robot.

In just two years, Gerald Proctor had been appointed President of SIES. This Gerald Proctor was nothing like the man that had picked up a book, read it and had an epiphany. Dictatorial, confident, and driven he was obsessed with the theory that Earth would be destroyed in one-hundred and fifty years. There were various theories about what would transpire when the Universe entered the Dark Energy age. Gerald was convinced the direst predictions were the most accurate. As he gained power and prestige, he led SIES on a clandestine path to develop a spacecraft, encased in a protective capsule surrounding an isolated universe. The capsule would have osmotic properties that could selectively be changed to allow enough radiation and other gases in space to enter and leave. This all could be controlled by the scientists residing in the spacecraft. Because of this design, the capsule and ship were constructed with the ability to survive as an exotic mass. It could travel at the speed of light. Thus, the most brilliant minds and a few select leaders could arrive at Indigo-35 and establish the new earth. First there would be a test mission to verify the existence of water on the planet and its ability to support life. At a secret location, deep within a mountain range in Switzerland, space craft and a protype of the land rover that would gather information from Indigo-35 were being designed.

Richard Quincy was extremely good at playing the odds, tiptoeing along the ethical fence, occasionally leaning toward the darker side. His charismatic ability of persuasion helped to build his kingdom and obese fortune. He could be both charming and intimidating, accommodating and manipulative. When Wilson contacted Richard about the investment opportunity with SIES, he told him that he needed the Indigo-35 project to move forward. The Foretell Bill for funding would have credence if things were moving forward at a faster pace. Richard saw an opportunity to maintain or even increase his wealth. If there was a planet that possibly could support life, he wanted to make sure that he had a way to exit the planet Earth should it continue to destroy itself in his lifetime. The Mars exploration project had suffered from the government's erratic dance with its funding. Though a potential crew had been chosen for a 2025 date to start a colony on the red planet, it was looking less promising that goal would be reached. Gerald gave Wilson some information he could use that supported his Bill. SIES was working on surface technology to improve selectivity in living cells. The funding from the Bill could expand the research into inventing a surface to surround spacecraft so that it could survive missions to and perhaps beyond Mars.

Wilson met with Gerald and Richard shortly after the meeting at D'Amato's. "Congress always wants to know if they are getting a good bang for their buck. How far along is SIES in the development of a surface shield for spacecraft?" Wilson asked Gerald. Richard leaned forward chewing on his expensive Haitian cigar.

"The ecologists have discovered the pollution of our waterways and soil is partly due to the farmers' use of pesticides that leach into the land and eventually contaminate the water. Developing a substance that can differentiate between plant, soil and living organisms would only allow the chemicals and nutrients into the cells of the pests that ravage the plants not invade the plants and soil as it does now. If that prototype is successful, the same process can be applied to building spacecraft and surface rovers in order to explore other planets in our solar system." Gerald explained. What Gerald did not share was that he and another scientist, Wayne Romer, had already developed a prototype for the land rover and were planning to be two of the "chosen" to leave the Earth and establish a colony on Indigo-35 while the Earth was evaporating. They were relying on the substance technology to be created by SIES technicians. They planned to bombard it with laser beams and use it to cover the spacecraft and the land rovers. They had estimated the journey would take five light years while Earth would have aged twenty-five years. They had to be able to travel eight times the speed of light. If the land rovers sent information back to the ship that supported the existence of water on the planet, they would land the spaceship and go about building a new Earth. Gerald would go down in history as the courageous hero he envisioned himself to be.

Emily was lonely. She missed her former home, her friends and the husband she had loved for many years. The Gerald Proctor she lived with now barely paid any attention to her or their children and families. She had anything money could buy, but that did not make her happy. The more her husband climbed the ladder in SIES, the less she saw him or knew him. She had tried everything. She made it a point to ask him how his day went in the first couple of years after he took the position. At first, he would share with her the exciting research they were doing and how much better he felt about himself having taken the risk. He spent more time at the office, answered less and less of her questions, and pulled away from sharing anything she was doing. The few hours he spent at home were gobbled up with phone conversations and computer work. They barely ate meals together and the sexual joy they had once shared was no longer available. She still loved him but living in the same house with a stranger was getting to be unacceptable. She had a profession which she had put on hold to raise the children. In fact, her job as a reporter for a local newspaper in Allentown, Pennsylvania was how she met Gerald Proctor.

Her assignment was not one of her favorites. Her boss wanted to do a series on the cost of Pharmaceuticals. He had arranged a series of interviews with the President of Ascot Pharmaceuticals, their Regional Research Coordinator and some of the technicians working in the laboratories. The initial interview with Wayne Romer had been interesting. It seemed like he wanted to make sure people knew why he earned his $800,000 salary and bonuses. Touting his multiple degrees and accomplishments he spent most of the interview patting himself on the back. The second interview was with Gerald Proctor, the Research Coordinator. Emily was mesmerized by this handsome man and his humility. He gave credit to his staff for the many cancer drugs that had been approved and marketed by Ascot, instead of highlighting his contributions. The feeling was mutual. Gerald was equally taken with the auburn-haired reporter who seemed genuinely interested in the company's research. There were very few people able to understand the highly technical lingo and dry rhetoric coveted by the scientists and technicians. Emily seemed genuinely taken with the subject. The group of articles she wrote for the paper were excellent. Emily's boss promoted her to lead investigative journalist and Gerald swept her off her feet during the year's courtship. They were married in 1974 and lived a wonderful life until Gerald read that awful book that changed everything.

"Gerry, I want to go back to work. There is so little to do around the apartment. I need to fill my time with something rewarding and substantial." Emily had bolstered the courage to talk to her husband in one of the rare dinners they ate together. She had made his favorites, stuffed cabbage, broiled red skin potatoes and pineapple upside-down cake. She waited as he stared at the laptop, which seemed glued to his hands.

After several minutes she closed his laptop, almost smashing his hand inside. "What are you doing, woman?!" he looked at her with disgust.

"I am talking to you, Gerald. We never communicate anymore. I am so unhappy. I have lost you to that mistress of a job of yours!" She tried to hold back the tears.

"I don't know what you are talking about. We talk… I give you this beautiful apartment and anything you want to buy." He started to open the computer.

Emily grabbed the computer, stood, and threw it across the room. "You don't even listen to me or make love to me. We don't have a marriage anymore. We are roommates – not even the relationship of a roommate. We are strangers sharing the same living quarters!" Emily sat back in the chair and sobbed.

Gerald walked over to the computer and stared at its broken screen. "Look what you have done! Go…. get out if you are so unhappy. I have important work… I'm going to be famous! Don't you think it is enough that I provide for you?"

Emily wiped her face, drenched with tears, and stared at him. She shook her head and walked to the bedroom, grabbed two suitcases out of the closet and began to through her clothes into them. The ache in her chest was like a vice closing so tight she could barely breathe. She heard the door slam and ran into the living room. Gerald was gone. Her marriage was over. Her heart was broken.

When Gerald returned from walking around the block, he found the note on their bed Emily had left.

Dear Gerry,

You have been the light of my life for so many years. I don't know how you could have changed so much that I no longer am part of your life anymore. I am going to my mother's in upstate New York. If you want to divorce me, our life together and our children's lives, I will have to live with that. I pray that you will come to your senses and don't lose everything for which you have always stood. I will always love you. My mother's address is in the book in the nightstand if you need to reach me. Please remember that wonderful man I met when I interviewed him. He was the best of you.

Love,
Emily

Gerald sat on the bed his hands shaking holding the letter. A small voice inside him tried to get his attention. *Go to her! Tell her you love her!* He sat there for several hours trying to justify in his mind who he had become. The sun rose over the city, He watched the miracle of a ball of radiation and fire fill the smog-laden sky. That part of him that needed to make a mark in history pushed away the yearning for Emily, for his loved ones. He crumpled up the letter, threw it into the trash can, showered and dressed in his SIES suit of armor and closed the door on his way to work on his quest to save the human race, or at least the best human minds.

Gerald had kept in touch with Wayne Romer, the President of Ascot Pharmaceuticals. Wayne had retired from the company in 2018. He still was a young man, fifty-two years old, when he retired. He was far from ready to become an armchair resident, pilfering hours in his garden and watching birds attack the feeders. Gerald needed someone who thought the way he did about science and had a similar affection for space travel. Though Gerald had disagreed with Wayne's focus on personal power and money when he was young, the magnetism of fame and recognition he felt he deserved transformed Gerald into the man he was now. Gerald hired Wayne to work as a consultant for the Indigo-35 project. Gerald and Wayne were the only ones who knew what the actual goal of the project was. Wayne was also a good friend of Vincent D'Amato. Vincent's conscience was a little left of center when powerful people asked for a favor. He rationalized that some shadiness was needed in order to gain favor with those in charge and those that held the purse strings of the country. When Wayne asked Victor to place a recording device under the plates of persons whose conversation was useful, he agreed for the price of $3000 per instance. Who would suspect? He did not want to have any knowledge of what those conversations were or what was being done with the conversations. He only was performing a service. Wayne wanted to make sure he could trust Gerald. He monitored the conversations of the two prime investors, Eddleman, and Quincy. to make sure they were not aware of the actual project's goal.

Emily spent two months at her mother's home recovering from the destruction of her marriage. She cried for an entire week, binged on potato chips and wine, signed divorce papers reluctantly and accepted her mother's tender loving care. When there were no more tears left, she took the advice of her two boys and her mother to blaze a new path. She sent resume's to newspaper editors in the New York and Pennsylvania area. She wanted to move to Easton, Pennsylvania which would be about an hour from New York City and the rent was less than most other areas – about $1250 per month. The stone that resided in her heart from the loss of her marriage grew into a mountain of determination. If she could somehow find out what this project was that had turned her husband into a robot, she might find some peace and satisfaction. Her prayers were answered when she received a letter from the New York Times interested in setting up an interview. She cut her hair, bought a very conservative blue suit, replaced her contact lenses with eyeglasses that made her look intellectual for the interview. The editor, William Churney, was impressed with her resume' and her history with Gerald. The Times had not been able to gain a meeting or even a phone conversation with this genius who had made monumental strides in chemicals' ecological effects and issues with the environment. Though Emily was honest about the trajectory of their marriage, she assured Mr. Churney that she would find a way to gain access to her Ex should she be hired.

──────── ◂ ◂ ✕ ▸ ▸ ────────

Erin met with Madeline and the other members of I-35H team at her apartment. Henry, Madeline and Martin each arrived at different times. They walked from different directions to the back entrance to Erin's apartment building. Their paranoia was mounting as they became suspicious when Nitrogen levels vacillated and the pressure to complete the surface agent project grew. The entire way SIES monitored their technicians, the strict rules and particularly the oversite by 0-10, 0-11, 0-12 and 0-13 robots was difficult to understand.

"I have the packet of garments we all have to wear at work. I understand that most all research entities require protective covering, but not ones that contain something that can read one's mind." Madeline started to unseal the package she had pilfered.

"Stop!" Henry exclaimed. "Suppose there is a device somewhere in there and it can send information back even when we are outside of the lab."

"You are right for a change," Madeline quipped. "Remember that music seems to interrupt the signal. Erin, can you put some music on while we open this thing?" Erin went over to her CD player and chose a disc by Nat King Cole.

"Maybe his soft voice will relax us. I know we are all nervous about this." Madeline carefully opened the packet and took out the coveralls, shoe covers, head cover, masks, and goggles. Each one of the team took an article and began to use their forensic talents examining them. After an hour, several glasses of wine and a pizza Erin had popped in the oven Martin quietly hushed everyone. Showing what he had discovered while examining the goggles through a magnifying glass, he gingerly took tweezers and pulled out a filament that was impregnated in the rim of the goggles. After removing it from the goggles he cautiously tucked it into a flash drive, placed it into a reading port of his computer. On the screen a myriad of numbers in various sequences appeared on the screen. They all looked at each other. There seemed to be a huge amount of information on Pod thirteen's filament. They wondered if it held all of his thoughts transposed into a code. Henry was the expert on decoding as he had been a technical operations' Corporal in the service. It took him another hour to crack the code.

"You see there is a cadence to the groups of numbers and letters in the code. The tangential fourth digit marks the beginning of another thought." He proudly explained.

"We have no idea what you just said, Henry, but I'm sure it is important." Madeline jabbed him as usual. He gave her his most egregious look.

"Well, aside from your insistent gouging, I think I can set up a translator in about thirty minutes."

"That is great, Henry. Go for it." Erin motioned to Madeline to shush.

When Henry had completed the translation, the group was utterly confused. Pod thirteen technician appeared to be working on the same project that Erin's Pod eighteen was assigned. His thoughts mirrored the same concerns about the miniscule rise in Nitrogen levels and the urgency to complete the project that Erin's team members expressed. One thing that was interesting was the formulas for pesticides were unfamiliar to any of them. The reason for the slight change in Nitrogen levels was explained as negligible, but thirteen still had concerns, especially when he and one of the other members of the Pod became ill.

"I wonder if all the Pod technicians are working on the same project. It doesn't make sense. That is a lot of brain power just to find a substance to protect cells against pesticides. Henry, can you or Martin see if you can find these two compounds anywhere. NH_3AgPP_7, NH_4AgPP_8 are not in the chart of elements, Nitrogen, Hydrogen and Silver are, but what is PP7 and PP8?" Erin asked. Henry and Martin perused Erin's library of chemistry books, atomic energy periodicals and heated up the keyboard on the computer for the next two hours. Madeline used her clearance at NASA to make inquiries from people she could trust about the two odd chemical abbreviations.

It was 11:00 pm when Madeline and Henry both shouted, "Oh my God! NASA had encountered a strange scattering of atoms sent back by the Martian rover about a year ago." These atoms occurred in clumps the size of a single atom. They seemed to possess the same properties of an exotic mass, which was impossible. Investigation into the very remote possibility of there being such an aberrancy had been unsuccessful. The research had gotten lost in the more evidence-based information sent back from the rover. The mass was labeled PP7, and curiosity diminished to a few paragraphs in volumes of reports documented about the Mars project. There were many questions about the entire project, but Erin pointed out they needed to focus on discovering a way to block their thoughts being kidnapped by 0-10. If they could accomplish that tonight, they would be able to look into the other discoveries while at work. Erin surmised that there were key words and phrases that triggered the filament to alert the captains of an inappropriate thought. It seemed that any thoughts with the words "space", "healthcare", "suspect", "suspicion" and other phrases would ping the brain of the captains and cause them to reprimand the member or members of a team not to follow the idea. Hopefully, no one had discovered a uniform packet had been taken from Pod thirteen.

"The design of the transmission system is most likely based on electroencephalogram patterns. Suppose one of us is attached by electrodes to a computer download of an EEG monitor. We make flash cards of the key words and phrases. The subject's auditory and visual centers in the brain would be isolated and the electrical signals transmitted to the EEG graph." Martin proposed.

"That sounds like it might work, Martin." Erin commented. "Are we all in agreement?" Madeline and Henry agreed to try the experiment. Henry was chosen to be the subject because he had the shortest hair. Petroleum jelly was used as it had the same properties as the conductive gel used in EEG labs. Erin found some wristwatch batteries in her jewelry box. She taped computer wires to them and placed them on Henry's scalp. Madeline found a website that allowed transmission of EEG patterns using telemedicine technology, which was in its early stages at that time. Henry put on the goggles containing the filament. Erin held up the flash cards containing the key words and phrases for Henry to concentrate on as he read them aloud. After an hour Erin had printouts of the EEG patterns produced when Henry's thoughts focused on the flash cards. The filament was removed from the goggles and fed into a zip drive. Madeline was able to visualize the filament's tracings. She matched it with Henry's EEG tracings and was able to substitute key phrases and words for the ones that spiked on the filament tracing. The next problem was how were they going to exchange the ghost filament for the ones impregnated in a new set of goggles each day. It was midnight. The team members were exhausted but also excited. The I-35 project had been riddled with failures because of limited access to chemicals, the constrictive interference of 0-10 and the constant downplay of minute changes in Nitrogen levels by SIES.

Madeline had the only unmonitored free time with the authorized exercise breaks that had been approved for her back problem. The group would use the musical override until she took her first walk in the morning. Each team member would remove the filament from their glasses and hand it to her when she passed. They had taken the filaments from the previous day to Erin's apartment and reprogrammed them with the overrides.

Madeline would place the original filaments she collected, wrap them in foil and place them in her brassiere. The aluminum in the foil would prevent the extracted filament from being detected as it was smuggled out of the lab.

Indigo-35 is a planet that was discovered several years ago along with four others light years away. It is slightly larger than Earth. It is located at the edge of the Universe and appears to be in a "Goldilocks zone"; the same distance from its star(sun) as Earth is from its sun. It has a rating of 0.88 out of 1.2 as to its comparison to properties similar to Earth's. The difficulty in being able to explore the planet's surface and atmosphere is that it is forty-five light years away from Earth. Any spacecraft would have to enter a wormhole in order to survive negative gravity propelling it at or greater than the speed of light (186,000 miles per hour). Wormholes exist throughout space, but Scientists had been unable to photograph or visualize them by instruments or satellites because they are very unstable. Einstein's theory of relativity supports the existence of negative gravitational forces needed to maintain the opening in the neck of the cylindrical wormhole. Gerald Proctor became obsessed with the theory that Earth entering the Dark Age might only have one-hundred and fifty years or less to exist before radiation from the sun would melt the surface and disintegrate the planets. He proceeded to hire seventy-two brilliant minds to staff a laboratory dedicated to the creation of a surface agent that could encompass a spacecraft's own universe and withstand the force of a negative gravitational environment. A similar substance could also be used to protect specially designed rovers to be used to explore Indigo-35, sending back information to confirm the existence of life forms and habitability of the planet. Gerald and Wayne had stumbled on what appeared to be a wormhole while they were going through images of space during an eclipse of the sun.

Gerald expanded an image he thought to be one of the many explosions from the sun's surface causing an irregular projection of the eclipse. On closer inspection the irregular image seemed to have irregular borders that undulated similar to the pseudopods of amoebas. Within these unusual perimeters a vacant, dark area appeared for a millisecond in three of the frames. There was no documentation of the phenomenon in any of the detailed reports of the sightings. Under the guise of discovering a protective barrier for plant cells, Gerald would be using the process to construct a shell that could survive the exotic mass negative gravity within the wormhole. The spacecraft and this structure was to be constructed in a remote mountain range in Switzerland. He would hand pick the scientists and aerospace personnel to take this uncharted journey. He, of course, would be one of them. He calculated that the planet being forty-five light years from Earth would require the ship to travel 8.5 times the speed of light so that the crew would only age five years by the time they reached Indigo-35's atmosphere. There was no guarantee that the planet would support life, nor that there would be human inhabitants. It was imperative he kept the actual project secret. He had to include Wayne as he would be needed in the actual construction. Wayne had paid one of the chefs at D'Amato's to plant a recording device under Senator Eddleman's and Richard Quincy's plates. Wayne wanted to make sure they hadn't become suspicious about the use of their investment.

CHAPTER V

APELLONAUTS

They were thousands of years ahead of Earthlings in technological advances. Apellonauts originally were life forms that resembled primates but had exceptional intelligence, the ability to reproduce telepathically and amazing dexterity because of the twelve digits on each hand. They focused on developing artificial intelligence that had the ability to make its own decisions, advance rapidly in any scientific venue with diminished emotional attachment. These aliens felt that emotions inhibited advancement. Indigo-35 had supported the early life forms ability to breathe by a mesh of tubes inside the chest that converted the high Nitrogen content of Indigo's atmosphere into a compound known as NPP. PP was Polyprotanium Phosphate, an element specifically found on the distant planets at the periphery of the Universe. When combined with the Carbon Dioxide within the Apellonauts' body it supported metabolism and respiration. The primate needed only to breathe three times in a twenty-four-hour period. The being could breathe at any altitude on Indigo's rocky surface as well as below the surface and in the liquid substance found in its lakes. The chemical make-up of the liquid on the planets in this zone was a group of hydrocarbons and nitrogen oxides. This created a liquid substance thicker than the H2O on Earth. The Apellonauts developed AI beyond their expectations. For the past one-hundred earth years (one year on Indigo was equal to one-hundred twenty earth days) the AI became so independent it replaced the original life forms. One day and night on Indigo was equal to fifty-two earth hours. The robots that replaced primate-like life were so far advanced that there would be no comparison to Earth's technology presently. The AI Apellonauts no longer needed a high concentration of nitrogen to support them. The PP, though, was necessary to keep their intricate internal components from the corrosive effect of the nitrogen. PP was only found in volcanic structures deep below the surface of the planet and in the atmosphere when the structures erupted. The aliens had been able to secure information about other planets for many years. There was little interest in Earth as the beings there seemed very primitive in their scientific advances, until recently. The cities beneath the surface of Indigo-35 (Apello) were becoming overpopulated despite leaders decreasing the manufacture of new AI aliens. It was determined that they would need to find a way to exist on the surface of the planet. This required decreasing the Nitrogen content of the atmosphere from 90 % to 78%. This would also allow a decrease in the amount of PP needed for the survival of the robotic population. The planet known as Earth had an atmosphere containing a consistent percentage of Nitrogen of 78%. They needed to harvest this element from Earth and bring it back to Indigo for study. They were confident they could create a radiological bombardment of their atmosphere to stabilize the earthly form of the element. No one on Earth had proven there were other forms of life in the Universe or that the sightings of UFO's were actually spacecraft from other planets spying on the Earth. There had been photographs of what some scientists believed to be alien spacecraft, but no solid proof that they existed. Several exploratory Apellonaut spacecraft zipped in and out of other planets' galaxies gathering information about them and other space objects. The advanced technology could build spaceships and space stations that could locate and move in and out of wormholes, avoid huge asteroids and other space debris and gather information from planets and galaxies.

Alterations in Earth's nitrogen cycle would disrupt ecosystem functions, increasing the risk of parasitic and infectious diseases for humans and wildlife. Already consequences of human activities had attacked the global Nitrogen cycle. The other forms of intelligence racing about the Universe rarely became aggressive or territorial. Those forms that harbored emotions such as anger, greed, jealousy, and resentment were changed or eliminated by more advanced forms that found that these emotions hindered progress. The microscopic green particles sent by the Apellonauts to Earth had one mission. Attach to enough Nitrogen atoms to be studied and converted by a radiological storm that decreased the atmospheric content to 78%. Over the past two years the atmospheric Nitrogen content on Earth was decreasing and increasing erratically by .0001% each year. This change was noticed by the ecologists and other scientist observing and studying climate change. They continuously warned the population of these concerns. Most of the warnings fell on deaf ears. A decrease was affecting the production of amino acids vital to proteins supporting life. An increase could become toxic to the respiratory and cardiac systems of humans. Increasing levels would enhance asthmatic symptoms, heart disease and cancer. The aliens had discovered a way to utilize the excess concentrations to stabilize the changes in Nitrogen levels in the Earth's atmosphere. Thus, the aliens would be less apt to be discovered. An interesting side effect of this stabilization procedure piqued their curiosity about Earthlings.

Erin's team I-35H filled their thoughts with formulas and process related information to their assigned SIES project. Madeline had exchanged her filament for the override model. She pretended to wipe off the lens of her goggles and slip the new filament created at Erin's apartment into her pair. She proceeded with her exercise walk around the lab. Assured that the Captains were not watching her, she slipped back into Pod thirteen's dressing area using the code she had memorized, interrupted the automatic light and motion detector alarm, took the elevator, and placed the packet of uniform articles back in its place. She slipped back into the main area and resumed her walk. She watched for any Captain approaching her Pod while the rest of the team exchanged filaments. If she noticed a Captain near Pod eighteen during the exchange, she would fake a fall or another diversionary tactic. When she arrived back at the Pod, all the original filaments would be wrapped in the foil and stuffed into her brassiere. The filament exchanges would be repeated each day. The team members hoped that they could pull this off without being discovered.

Henry couldn't stop his concern over the minute fluctuations in atmospheric Nitrogen pumped into their Pod. The Nitrogen was used in compounds the team was trialing to finalize the project. It was stored in cylinders as were other gaseous elements needed for their research. The rebound effect of the Apellonauts' extraction caused nitrogen levels to fluctuate erratically. Physicians noticed increases in some chronic conditions and intermittent bouts of viral epidemics. Pod twelve and thirteen technicians had not returned to work. It had been over a week since they became ill. When Madeline took her exercise walks past the other Pods, she noticed their computer screens appeared to contain the same formulas as her own Pod. She didn't linger long enough to observe more critically. She didn't want to be questioned by the Captains or to risk losing her exercise privileges. Henry and Martin believed that there were other life forms in the Universe and that there were intelligent beings observing Earth and other constellations. Erin and Madeline were not convinced though they had not totally ruled out the possibility.

◄ ◄ ✖ ► ►

Emily Proctor had covered several local and State political and health issues in her first six months with the New York Times. She watched for any information coming in on the wire service about SIES or the administrators. Since the divorce neither Emily nor her boys had any communication with their father. They all had tried to keep in touch with him, but he rarely responded. The financial settlement-alimony and gifts to his two sons and their families had been generous. Emily and the rest of the family was heartbroken over the radical change in this wonderful man. Emily hoped to be given an assignment to interview the gurus of SIES NY. There was a press conference being held by Senator Wilson Eddleman to garner support for a Bill that had passed House of Representatives approval and was going to the Senate in the next two weeks. The request was to fund research to produce a substance that could coat cells allowing only certain chemicals or atoms to reach those cells. Pesticides would be allowed to enter the cells of parasites and insects but be kept away from plant cells or the soil. This concept, known as osmotic selectivity, could be applied to spacecraft and make possible distant space exploration. Perhaps this was the research that had mesmerized Gerald. She knew he was deeply concerned about the state of the planet. He rallied vehemently for tactics to address climate change as well as efforts to explore distant planets and stars beyond Mars. Her love for him had been challenged. She still held a special place in her heart for the man. Emily's chance came when her boss mentioned to his investigative journalist team that he needed someone to cover the press conference. Senator Eddleman, Gerald Proctor, CEO of SIES, and two other experts were to appear in two days on National TV channels at a press conference narrated by a famous talk show host, Arthur Ash. Emily enthusiastically volunteered to cover the event.

She wore her most flattering business suit, styled her hair so it gently touched her shoulders and framed her face. Her make-up accented her sparkling blue eyes and highlighted her fine features. The studio at KWC TV was filled with journalists from other newspapers, ecologists, environmentalists, cameramen, Secret Service Men, producers, make-up crew and equipment. The participants, Senator Eddleman, Richard Quincy (the billionaire), Dr. Gerald Proctor, CEO SIES, and Dr. Wayne Romer (Former Professor MIT and Scientist for a large Pharmaceutical company), and an Advisory Council representative from the US Aerospace Program took their seats. Arthur Ash joked with them for a few minutes. When the "roll" call began the program, he morphed into the distinguished, austere interviewer he portrayed to his TV audience. The bright lights gave three-dimensional depth to the speakers sitting at a curved desk with a blue sky portrayed in the background. The conference began after introductions by Ash, with Senator Eddleman summarizing the major points of the Bill. Richard explained in his charming way the financial benefits of the project and Wayne attempted to explain in lay terms the possible uses to enhance space exploration. Gerald looked older and much thinner since she had last seen him. He was still handsome and portrayed confidence and respect for the other participants. He focused on the main research being paramount to protect plant life, the soil, and the atmosphere. At this time radiation, space debris and gravitational forces prevented spacecraft and exploratory equipment from venturing beyond Mars. He emphasized it would be years to test the results once a substance was tested on the planet's needs, let alone attempting to adapt it for space exploration. This is why funding was critical in the long term. Richard had generously donated funds to keep the research progressing. The Federal funds requested in the Bill would allow that research to expand to other genres.

Emily sat near the back of the room. Her heart rate quickened when Gerald spoke. The questions from the press and other participants in the audience had been inciteful and non-confrontational. She raised her hand, and the moderator acknowledged her.

"The lovely lady in the back of the room. Miss...?" Arthur prompted.

"Emily Proctor, New York Times," she said. An uncomfortable buzz rose from the audience at her name. Emily stood as tall as her small frame allowed and did not let on that she was at all disturbed by the rustle. "Thank you. My question is for Dr. Proctor. Doctor, are you concerned that there have been reports of irregularities in the levels of Nitrogen in our air?" she looked intently at Gerald. There was a pregnant pause when Gerald realized it was his Ex-wife asking the question. A myriad of feelings rushed into his gut, and he had to catch a few breaths before he answered.

"Ms. Proctor, good to see you. We monitor those fluctuations closely. They appear consistent with broader climate change patterns."

Scientists and Environmentalists monitor these types of phenomenon closely. There has been some success in this area. It takes people and industry all over the world cooperating to eliminate these damaging results of global warming."

Emily thanked him. Her legs felt like mush. She was praying no one heard her plop back into her chair. After the press conference she attempted to leave as fast as possible. She knew she should join the throng of journalists in the hallway outside the studio to talk with the other panel members. As she bent to pick up her notebook and purse, she turned to exit, and he was standing in front of her.

"Ems, you look wonderful! You are working for the Times. That is terrific! How are the kids?" Gerald was so close to her she felt the warmth of his body.

"Scott has a little boy, Darrin, two years old and adorable. He is remarkably successful in a large law firm and a great father and husband." She didn't mean it as a jab at her Ex. Her cheeks were on fire. Gerald's shoulders drooped and he looked down at the floor. "David is still single. He works endless hours at Mayfield Pediatric Hospital. He is a particularly good Pediatrician; loves those kids. You should call them, Gerry. They miss you."

"I…I am so sorry for letting my work push away my family. I'll be sure to call them. Are you...ahem…are you…have you..." he stammered.

"No, Gerry. I'm not. I'm too busy trying to succeed in this "man's world" to date." Emily bit her tongue. She just wanted to get out of there. The room had gotten quite hot, though most of the people and staff had left.

Gerald reached hesitantly for her shoulder. "Ems, I'm so sorry I hurt you." His hand melted into her jacket. She wanted to fold up into those long arms.

Emily moved away from him and headed for the double doors leading to the reception area. "Me too, Gerry….me too." She tried not to stumble as she rushed past the crowd. Tears burned her eyes as she rushed to her car, climbed in and closed the door.

Hospitals were beginning to see an increase in admissions for severe asthma attacks, re-occurrences of cancer in patients deemed cancer free for years, heart problems and pneumonia. Nitrogen levels continued to fluctuate erratically between 70 to 90%. Farmers worried when their crops withered despite no change in the soil or rainfall. Ecologists and Infectious Disease experts had not been able to find an answer to the changes. Minute fluctuations of elements in the atmosphere could be explained by the effects of global warming but not to this degree.

Six months after Erin began working in the SIES laboratory team they had a breakthrough. A formula they had been working on combining Nitrogen, Hydrogen and Beryllium were subjected to laser beams to produce clumping of the atoms. The resulting substance tested positive for osmotic selectivity, that product also mimicked exotic matter (dark matter) even when bombarded with high doses of radiation, extreme heat and extreme cold. The substance, which they named E-Hydroxynitrate (EHN22), was tested for strength, resilience, and osmotic selectivity. When Gerald and Wayne were notified by 0-10 of the experiment, they made an unprecedented visit to the laboratory. Erin and her teammates were excited about the discovery. They had been able to carry out their filament exchanges without apparent exposure. The announcement of the top brass visit changed the lunch schedule and also Madeline's exercise routine. They would have to cover any thoughts that would cause suspicion with the musical override. Henry's concern over the Nitrogen fluctuations deepened as the team worked with the instability of that element critical to the formula. Using spectral analysis (an instrument that analyses frequencies to determine the power density of a random process) Henry and Martin were puzzled with a hazy blue beam intermittently appearing near the canisters containing Nitrogen. They had never seen anything like it before. It had a ghostlike, insubstantial quality, and the spectral analysis printout showed no record of its presence Was there some kind of energy able to penetrate the thick walls and monitoring systems of the laboratory without detection? They were stumped and vowed to find a way to track the beams after the executive's visit.

Gerald Proctor and Wayne had dressed in the uniform all the technicians and Coordinators wore. Their goggles were designed differently from the teams' goggles. They had wider rims and the lenses were coated with a light pink tinge. Erin pushed her observation of the goggles out of her thoughts by a raucous rendition of "Flight of the Bumblebee" by an orchestra. Her other teammates did a similar cover-up. Henry and Wayne did not mention their discovery of the blue beam or their concerns over Nitrogen fluctuations.

We are very pleased with the results of your hard work," Gerald commented. "If the remainder of your testing proves to have the excellent results you have obtained so far you will be given a two-week paid vacation in Switzerland. All expenses will be taken care of by SIES. Hope you all like skiing." Gerald surveyed the team members to see their reaction. Erin and Madeline were noticeably excited. Henry and Martin seemed less enthused. "If there are any reasons why you are unable to accept the gift you will need to let your Captain know ASAP. Should you accept the prize you will be assigned to another area of research here at SIES NY. The aerospace department will be working on the development of food substances and packaging that would be used in the Mars exploration project planned for 2025." That part of the announcement touched the enthusiasm button in Henry and Martin. Thoughts of working with NASA and other aerospace scientists pushed out concern over some unexplained beam.

The Apellonauts sent to extract Nitrogen atoms from Earth's atmosphere were near to realizing the goal to combine elements to produce Nitrogen levels of 78%. In another Earth-time week some would be returning through the wormhole back to Indigo-35 while other ships remained to observe Earth. The research robots on the planet would begin to develop a process to bombard their atmosphere with radiation forcing the Nitrogen levels to combine with PP at the desired 78%.

Gerald and Wayne spent the rest of the day following their visit to SIES laboratory programming their captains to direct the other seventeen Pod teams to utilize the formulas from Pod eighteen. They were convinced that the testing was already adequate to have a substance they could use to build the spacecraft and exploratory roamers for the journey to Indigo-35. They planned to have the I-35H team go to Switzerland to work on the spacecraft and rover, not for a vacation. They would decide who to bring along on the mission and who would be rendered amnesic. After the other Pod technicians completed manufacturing of EHN22 (EHydroxynitrate), those who would not be needed for the mission were subjected to a "brain drain" procedure where all memory of their stint with SIES would be erased.

They would be released back to their former lives unable to recall what had happened to the past year. Part of the re-programming would prevent all of those technicians from reporting amnesia to physicians or anyone else. They were to explain absences to their friends and loved ones as an assignment they were instructed never to reveal.

The Apellonauts began to notice increased amounts of Nitrogen being absorbed by the city of New York. They calculated mathematically the exact position of this disturbance and their programmed brain prompted them to investigate the reason it was occurring in one of the primitive buildings the earthlings had constructed. The language these beings spoke, and the electronic patterns emitted by some kind of organ in their tiny heads could be translated into computer language by the technology of the aliens. When it was learned that these earthlings were planning an expedition to their planet within the next earthling year, they reported back to the Apellonauts in charge of protecting the planet from invasion. The leaders of the Apellonauts were interested in studying these beings from Earth should they have enough intelligence to find a way to travel the extreme distances in time. The aliens extracting Nitrogen were programmed to absorb all conversations and thoughts from the beings in New York and a place known as Switzerland. This information was sent back to Indigo-35 so they could study it and prepare to welcome humans should they have the brain power to construct a spacecraft that could survive a wormhole. It would be an interesting diversion to examine primitive forms of intelligence.

Shipments of the new EHN22 were flown to the mountain lab in Switzerland. There were no questions from the officials in Customs as SIES had established businesses all over the world. Cannisters labeled with chemical formulas had been flown back and forth internationally by the company for years. Erin, Madeline, Henry, and Martin had shopped for skiing outfits and other new clothes for their "vacation". They were so excited they did not question the fact that their tickets were only one-way. 0-10 explained that was how all business travel at SIES, even the executives, was arranged. All travel was on a private SIES jet service, so round-trip arrangements were unnecessary. Henry felt more comfortable going on this trip since the Nitrogen levels seemed to have returned to normal and there were no other sightings of a "beam" with their instruments. The bonus they received was very generous. They were also given Swiss spending money while in the country.

The SIES jet was amazing. Plush couches, gourmet meals and an open bar added to the extravagant ambiance. They talked excitedly about taking tours, mountain climbing and skiing while they were in that beautiful country. Lulled by the surroundings, the almost soundless trip across the ocean, too much rich food and drinks they slept deeply, not even hearing the pilot announce "fasten seatbelts, please" for their descent into Geneva airport. When they awoke, they were in a suite of rooms on top of a mountain somewhere. There bags were unpacked, and contents placed neatly in closets and drawers.

"What happened? How did we land and get in this room without awakening?" Martin asked as he tried to shake off dizziness.

"Look at these mountains!! They are all around us. Where in the heck are we?" Henry plopped on one of ornate couches.

Erin shook her head as she was feeling woozy also. "I don't know. The last thing I remember was we were drinking a cocktail celebrating on the plane. I don't remember anything after that." Henry got up and was trying the two doors in the spacious suite. One of them led to a bedroom with a king-size bed covered with an elegant comforter and six fluffy colorful pillows. The other door led to two adjoining bedrooms. There was no other exit in either of the two bedrooms in the suite. Henry tried to loosen the knob on what appeared to be an exit door, but it wouldn't budge. There were no telephones anywhere and the window was locked as well with no visible way to open it. They all began to panic. This was no vacation.

Welcome I-35H Team. You probably wonder what is going on. SIES has given you the esteemed opportunity to work with us on the development of a spacecraft and exploration vehicles that will attempt a mission to planets far beyond Mars. Because of the nature of this project, you will be quarantined to the work areas inside this mountain and this suite. There is an exercise area with equipment for you to use as well as an Olympic size swimming pool in the lounge area of the work site. All communication devices have been removed from your personal luggage. You will be sent meals from the menus located on the desk in the living area of your suite. Wake-up is at 6:00 am every day. A guide will escort you to the work site at 8:00 am. You will each be given an assignment to be completed as directed. No information is to be given to the outside world as this would cause extreme panic. We do not want that. Your workday will commence at 4:00 pm every day. The television is equipped with any movie or show you wish to view. You will not be able to access any news programs. Do not attempt to rig any kind of communication device. You will be watched 24 hours a day. Please enjoy your stay.

The voice was the same as the one they heard every day in the anteroom while donning their uniforms at SIES Laboratories. While the voice was ranting on, all of the team members searched for listening devices, speakers, wires, anything. The voice, like the one at SIES, seemed to come from the walls themselves. They couldn't even write notes to one another as they were being watched. They were confused and frightened. How could they get out of this one?

The lab at SIES NY was remodeled into a large business office. The technicians who were not chosen to work on the space mission were rendered amnesic and sent on their way. Gerald and Wayne along with three of the brightest aerospace pilots from NASA flew into Geneva airport shortly before the plane with Team I-35H arrived. Two black SUV's left the airport for Chaine de Arivis mountain range, thirty miles outside of Geneva. They had no plans to return. They were committed to a mission that had no guarantee they would survive.

The alarm wakened the restlessly sleeping I-35H team. They had tried watching a movie while searching under tables, in drawers, in light fixtures for monitoring devices. Even though they were being watched, they had to do something.

The EHN22 substance had passed rigorous testing. It demonstrated resilience at extreme temperatures, flexibility under pressure, and the ability to change its osmotic selectivity—blocking or admitting gases, chemicals, and liquids as needed. EHN22 adhered to the shell of the spacecraft and the tubular structure that would contain the universe around the ship. The exotic matter created in the formula would allow the spacecraft and surrounding structure to pass through the wormhole forcing its neck to remain open. If this did not work, the spacecraft, capsule and man-made universe would be evaporated by the negative gravitational forces. The main spacecraft was shaped like a huge whale. The "mouth" or aft opening was as high as a ten-story building and as wide as a city block. This area would house the space station that would be placed in orbit near Mars. This would serve as an ejection point from which the spacecraft would launch into the wormhole when it appeared on the instruments. There would be less than thirty minutes to enter the wormhole and continue the voyage into space and time. It was difficult to verify the competency of this wormhole as it was unstable. Wayne had recorded observations of the wormhole's activity. After numerous sightings, the average amount of time the wormhole's mouth was visible was thirty minutes.

Erin and her teammates were assigned to stations inside and outside the three spacecraft being built to establish exact amounts of elements in the EHN22 substance before other workers on the site covered the spacecraft, technically advanced exploration rovers and the capsules. There was a team that worked in a huge bubble-like structure on the components of the spacecraft universe. None of the workers made eye contact with Erin or her teammates. When they communicated with other workers near them, it was with a small hand-held instrument, about the size of a walkie-talkie. Erin was allowed inside one of the ships. Just behind the room that would house the space station, there was a smaller room that would house the rover. The rovers were not like any Martin, or his teammates had seen at NASA. A cabin enclosed in a transparent shell housed a control panel and several computers. There was special seating inside the cabin. The controls connected to digging, sampling, suction, and laser artillery were attached to the sides of the machine. Instead of tires the rover would move about the terrain on treads similar to those on a war tank. Laser lighting fixtures surrounded the outer shell. Beyond the room that would house the rovers were the spaceship's control center and living quarters for the crew. The control center, constructed of twelve-inch-thick thermal plutonium and a windshield of the same transparent material used in the rover, rose on top of the spaceships' control rooms and the space that housed the rover. Living quarters were spacious and designed for comfort and efficiency. There were bedrooms, work-out rooms, a full laboratory, cafeteria, kitchen and lounge. The rest of the ship was where the engine, air control and fuel tanks were housed. Erin's team was only allowed in the lab, the control center and living area. All the other areas were inaccessible. The team was directed to verify fuel composition, pressure testing and competency of the capsule and spaceship's support systems. The only entrance and exit to the work area deep inside the mountain was from a shaft connected to a storage unit several yards from the living quarters for the workers. The living quarters appeared to be the elegant Chalet on one of the peaks of the mountain range. Gerald, Wayne and the flight crew slept on the main spacecraft. They wanted to mimic the life they would be experiencing during the five Earth years it would take to reach the galaxy near Indigo-35. Weightlessness was established inside the ship so that they could become accustomed to living and working in that element. Erin and Martin had tried an old system, similar to Morris Code, to communicate secretly. Blinking of the eyes, facial grimaces and repetitive taps on soft surfaces, such as couches did not seem to be noticed by the system spying on them. It seemed that the SIES spies had some respect for privacy. They tested trying to write messages with a bar of soap on the shower stall wall. There was no reprimand or questioning by "the voice" when they were performing personal tasks in the bathrooms regardless of their conversations or actions. One flaw. Now they needed to find other flaws so they could devise a plan to escape. How would they ever get off the mountain? They probably had been flown there in a helicopter. How did SIES get the materials to build the space stations, spaceships, and rovers? Since SIES owned a fleet of airplanes, the materials might have been air lifted and parachuted to the mountain top. The teammates took turns watching the sky out of the one window in their suite. They were sure the window was positioned in a way that viewing any activity around the area and aircraft in the sky was not able to be seen.

Gerald had kept his promise to Emily by contacting his sons and Scott's family members. He apologized fervently to them telling them he had been given exceedingly difficult assignments during his rise to high positions in SIES. He promised he would visit them soon. He sent gifts to them and post cards from other countries, except for when he was in Switzerland. One week before he took his last trip to that country, he visited Scott and his wife and grandchildren and David at his apartment near the hospital. Though his heart was heavy, knowing this was the last time he would see them, he acted jubilant and loving while he was there. He couldn't get Emily out of his mind, as much as he tried. Part of him wanted to capture her and take her with him on this adventure. He knew that was impossible. He called her after he had visited the kids. She, too, wanted to see him again. He seemed sad and preoccupied when he called her. It was probably this huge project. Somehow, she would find a way to see him. He told her that he always loved her.

The Apellonauts left two of their spacecraft and crew roaming around Earth and forwarding the progress of SIES's mission to Indigo-35. They were sure that Earth's primitive beings would not have the technological advances that Apello's (Indigo-35) inhabitants had. They could keep the wormholes through which they traveled open by a radioactive beam devised to magnetize energy creating a positive or negative gravitational imprint. When the neck of the wormhole was subjected to this beam, it would stay open and loose its destructive atom smashing ability long enough to allow their spacecraft to exit through time at a speed of 558,000 MPH, three times the speed of light. Aging was not a concern of the Apellonauts. For humans, their age would equal one year for every fifteen on Earth during the trips between galaxies and other journeys. The containers of Nitrogen extracted from Earth were placed in a launching apparatus, mixed with PP and fired into Apello's atmosphere. When the gas was released and bombarded with another type of radioactive beam, the levels changed to 78 %. The Apellonauts began to build some cities on the surface of the planet for the first time in hundreds of years. They continued to procreate in their unusual manner.

Erin and her teammates were amazed how advanced and efficient the actual Indigo-35 project was. They marveled at the size of the three spacecraft and how an area as large as a city had been excavated in the mountain to produce the work area. It had to have taken years and millions of dollars to accomplish what they had so far.

Henry wanted to be part of one of the missions, regardless of the danger and the finality of never being able to return to Earth. He had no real human attachments. He felt he could be useful on the mission because of his environmental background and having worked in the aerospace field. Martin also had a desire to be part of such a bold undertaking, though he was more hesitant than Henry. Madeline did have family back home. She was divorced but had a daughter and granddaughter that she couldn't imaging leaving forever. The scientific part of her yearned to explore and take risks, but not one as challenging as this. Erin felt her expertise was still valuable on Earth. Her planet needed experts to fight the battle against global warming and climate change. The Indigo-35 mission was enticing, but her heart was committed to saving her planet and the human race for as long as possible. The only way she could envision an escape from her present situation was to kidnap one of the rovers. How to accomplish that would depend on her teammates' cooperation.

Emily still had friends at SIES. Matt Fornier was the CFO of the company. He also had a Doctorate in Elemental Science, a Masters' degree in Chemical Engineering and a second Masters' degree in Finance and Health Administration. He and Emily had attended college together and had stayed in touch even after the divorce. One would never know the man with an uneven beard, a unibrow and ruddy complexion was a genius. He loved telling jokes and laughing at ones he had told over and over. He was mildly obese with a belly that would gyrate when he guffawed. He had worked with Gerald at the pharmaceutical company and in a private group of scientists consulting on aerospace projects at NASA. When Gerald began his rise in SIES he begged Matt to join the company to work on anti-pollution projects. His expertise in finance helped the company avoid two economic crises that might have put them out of business in several locations, including the home office in New York. He still had some involvement in the anti-pollution projects, but Gerald rewarded his saving the company by making him CFO. Matt was devastated when Gerald and Emily divorced. He had watched his friend spend most of his time at SIES or traveling for the company and less time with his family. He had even talked with Gerry to see if there was someone else in the company who could lighten his load. It was almost like a force beyond Gerald Proctor's control pulling him away from a personal life. Matt often found Gerry sleeping on the couch in his office and spending weekends planted in the laboratory or on a jet to who knows where.

When Emily called him and asked if he could meet her at a coffee shop near her home, he readily agreed. Matt had noticed in the reams of spreadsheets he perused each day the SIES jets had made several more trips to Geneva Switzerland than usual. Not only were their executive flights but also their commercial planes had been flying to a place several miles from the Geneva airport, landing to re-fuel within the same day and returning to LaGuardia airport. The cargo on those flights was listed only as "construction materials". There were no itemized lists of what type of materials were being transported. There was no record of building a SIES satellite in Switzerland, but there was a project called *Aravis Chalet* on the books about a year ago. Matt did not have any record of appropriations for a Chalet in Switzerland. He was puzzled and made a notation to ask Gerald about it when he returned from a business trip.

Emily was more beautiful than when he had seen her before the divorce. She was dressed in an expensive suit that complimented her shapely figure. Even in her 60's she was still striking. Besides the eye pleasing demeanor, she appeared more confident than he remembered. Matt sat across from her in a booth after a long hug.

"Thanks so much for meeting me, Matt. It's been a while. How are Linda and the girls? I feel so bad that we have lost touch." Emily sipped on her glass of ice water. Matt had ordered a beer.

"The kids and Linda are doing great. Ems, it is wonderful to see you. You look amazing! What have you been up to this past year?" Matt couldn't help noticing she still wore her wedding ring.

"I am writing a column with the New York Times, mostly about climate change. I'll get right to the point. I need to see Gerry. Something strange is going on with him. I talked with him about a month ago and he sounded depressed and apologetic, almost like he was going to vanish. I never stopped loving the Gerald I married and lived with for twenty-six years. When he took the job at SIES he started to change…I didn't know this Gerald anymore. Then I saw him at a press conference about the Finance Bill Senator Eddleman was sponsoring to help pay for a project called Indigo-35. I spoke with him for a few moments, and he was pleading me to forgive him, promising to contact the boys and almost like he was saying good-bye forever." Matt could see tears glistening in her eyes. She blinked them away and patted her eyes with her napkin. "How does he seem to you?"

"He has been strangely distant lately. I saw he was making quite a few trips out of town and even out of the country. When the Eddleman Bill passed he hardly went home. He was at the office or flying somewhere. I approached him about some construction project in Switzerland and he avoided answering. He even became angry with me, telling me it was personal project for investors, and I needn't worry about it. That is not like him. He has always been a stickler for documenting every penny. He has been gone over a week now and no one seems to know where he is."

"Oh, dear, Matt. Is there any way you can find out where he is? Has anyone tried to go to his townhouse and make sure something didn't happen to him.?" Emily's composure was wilting. She shredded the napkin and called the waiter over to order a Manhattan.

"I did ask one of my staff to check to see if any executive flights left in the past couple of weeks. There were two flights that were supposed to have landed in Rome, Italy but they must have been diverted to Geneva for some reason. The planes left within two hours of each other, and both were scheduled to arrive in Italy. They suddenly changed their destination and were seen on radar landing in Geneva. I have a suspicion Gerry was on one of those planes. I have tried to reach him. I have left messages and voicemails, but no answer. I'm even thinking of going to Switzerland myself. I went over to his house, and everything was locked up, no lights or sign of anyone there. I might have the police check it out to make sure nothing happened to him at home."

"Matt, I want to go with you. In my work at the New York Times as a reporter I have been assigned to follow SIES and its satellites around the world. I do think you should call the police to check his home. If you decide to go to Switzerland, can I go with you? I am really worried now. The kids said when he finally visited with him he seemed happy on the surface. They could detect a sadness underneath his jovial demeanor. They are worried too." Matt agreed to have Emily accompany him to Switzerland and also let her know what the police found, if anything, at his townhouse.

The spacecraft, rovers, artificial universe and capsule were ready. Supplies had been delivered by the air drop. The SIES transport planes had brought everything needed to realize Indigo-35 project. Gerald didn't want anyone snooping around the Chalet and the mountain range. He and Wayne had chosen this particular group of mountains because their difficult terrain and jagged rock formations were not a hot spot for skiers and mountain climbers. The few who had attempted skiing and climbing had not survived. Gerald was concerned that Matt, his friend and CFO, was questioning the expenses that weren't itemized in the financial statements. That was a radical difference from the way Gerald had demanded in the past. He had been a stickler for detail and documentation of every penny, a habit that intensified after Matt rescued SIES from bankruptcy.

Erin was getting pressured to complete the final battery of tests on the artificial universe that would surround the spacecraft and the EHN22 screens on the capsules, the spacecraft and rovers. The rovers' propulsion systems would be tested on a two-mile track constructed by one of the work teams. She was anxious as it was rumored that a target date for lift off was in the next ten days. What would happen to the workers after that? What would keep them from reporting what they had been working on? What had happened to the technicians at SIES NY? How would anyone get off the mountain and return back to the States? As "D-day" (Deployment Day) grew near, the crews of the three spacecraft, Gerald and Wayne met to address some of the same questions. The SIES NY lab techs who were not chosen for the Indigo project had been rendered amnesic about any of the work they had done in the lab. There were two options for keeping the mission secret; use the same "brain drain" technique for the workers at the launch site, most of which were technicians from the lab, and/or implode the work site along with the Chalet, burying all evidence in the mountain. None of the team scheduled to leave for Indigo-35 were murderers. They were hoping that the cave would eventually be discovered and used by future scientists. The Chalet was beautiful. Perhaps it could be used as a retreat center or a vacation spot for a millionaire willing to purchase it. Gerald had chosen several of the scientists and technicians who worked on the project, offering them a seat on the spaceships. They would have to understand once they left Earth, there would be little chance they would return. The risks and dangers needed to be understood. They would not be told that Gerald feared the destruction of Earth and several other planets might occur in the next one-hundred and fifty years. If that were known, they would want to bring their loved ones. It was settled. Their feelings were conflicted. They were excited about being part of a bold and dangerous journey in the name of science but filled with the sadness of leaving Earth and all the people they cared for. Perhaps people would take information they would learn about the Universe and other planets and apply it to saving their planet.

When Henry and Martin took the rovers for a test run, they noticed a couple of crevices in the mountain wall seeping water. They smuggled an endoscopic camera device on one of the test runs. The snakelike tubing with an internal camera at the tip was fed along the track made by the tiny waterfall. One exited several yards from the Chalet. Henry could see there was a flat surface large enough for a helicopter to land and a cement brick building at the edge of the site. Martin had traveled farther down the track to where they had discovered a second crack in the wall. He fed the device along the crack to an opening at the surface. The camera hung over a steep cliff that ended in a dark blue lake thousands of feet below the surface. There were cracks along the face of the cliff, signs of some instability in the mountain due to earthquakes or avalanches. Martin and Henry were not questioned about using the camera device as they had reported needing to investigate cracks in the rock. They did not report their actual discovery. When the I-35H team returned to their suite in the Chalet they took turns spending time in the bathrooms, not taking showers and primping, leaving messages on what they had found during the workday. Erin had watched small groups of workers taken to the areas deep within the mountain for meetings. Erin had been informed that her team was to meet with Drs. Proctor and Romer in two days.

I'm worried that they have discovered us communicating in these bathrooms and investigating things along the rover test track. Erin wrote in code on the walls of the shower. Henry paced back and forth in the bathroom. Erin tried to reassure him. *No reprimand yet. Maybe they will be telling us when we will leave here.*

They will not risk us talking about this mission. They will have to eliminate us. Henry wrote.

Will they take us with them on this mission? Martin wrote.

I will go if that is the alternative to being eliminated. Erin wrote hesitantly.

Matt and Emily boarded the SIES plane that next day after the police found no sign of Gerald at his home nor any sign of a disturbance. He had to be in Switzerland for whatever reason. They both wanted to know he was alive and to see if he would share why these lies and secrets. Neither of them felt like eating the delicious food or imbibing in the drinks offered on the flight. The flight attendant had not seen Gerald or Wayne on the flights she recently took with SIES planes. The last flight she was on several weeks ago had four passengers from the SIES laboratory in New York. The company had given them paid vacations in Switzerland for their work in an Indigo project. She remembered they had fallen asleep after some heavy drinking during the flight. She had left that plane to board another that was returning to the States. They were still snoozing when she left. Matt had not seen any requisitions for vacation vouchers for lab employees before he realized that Gerald was missing. Wayne Romer's department supervisor told Matt that Dr. Romer had taken several weeks off to go on a much-needed vacation. He had not revealed his destination. The supervisor was puzzled because this was out of character for the boss that usually micro-managed his aerospace department even when he was out of the office.

Emily tried once again to reach Gerald on his phone. She left a voicemail message to contact her, texted him and sent urgent messages to his e-mail. She told him Matt and she had located him being in Geneva and would he please contact them as they were very worried about him. Matt tried to contact Wayne on the same lines.

Gerald saw the text and e-mails from Emily at the same time Wayne received his. They wondered how they had found out they were both in Switzerland. This was not good. They had enough to deal with readying things for the mission. Now there were two people they cared for snooping around. They couldn't let them interfere with the mission. Timing was of the essence in order to arrive near Mars, eject the space station into orbit and be there when the wormhole appears. Gerald decided to e-mail Emily.

Ems, I am on a very important business trip in Germany. Wayne and I cannot share anything about this project with you or anyone else at SIES. We are both fine. Do not worry. As soon as we have things worked out with this deal we will return to the States and call you. Please go back home or ski or something.

Yours,

Gerry

Emily was relieved when she received the e-mail. Matt was even more puzzled. He had always been included in the projects at SIES, even the ones that had to be kept concealed for a period of time. He was able to track Gerry's GPS signal from the e-mail. It had come from a remote area thirty miles south of Geneva. There were very few towns in the area surrounded by the ominous Chaine de Aravis mountain range. Why would Gerry lie to them? Matt didn't want to frighten Emily with his suspicions. He arranged for separate hotel rooms for both of them. He told Emily he was going to the lounge for a drink and suggested she rest. He hoped he was convincing when he said he was going arrange for a SIES flight home the next day. Matt used the computer in the hotel to check out the location of Gerry's signal. There appeared to be a building on one of the highest peaks in the Aravis range. A SIES helicopter was scheduled to arrive the next morning in Geneva airport. He planned to get Emily on that flight back to the States using the excuse for his staying that he was going to track down Gerry and Wayne in Germany. He would promise to keep her informed.

The helicopter arrived at 8:00 am. The pilot agreed to take Emily back to the U.S. She tried to resist but Matt said it would be better if he met with Gerry without her there to stir up emotions. Emily begrudgingly boarded the helicopter. Matt waited until she was safely in the air then he rushed to retrieve a rental car he had reserved and headed for the mountain range. He had no idea what he would do when he got there. There had to be a way to get to the building on the peak.

The pilot of the helicopter did not know who Emily was. He knew Matt so he felt okay to transport her. There was a delivery he had to make about thirty miles south of Geneva. Some sort of a Chalet or hotel located in a weird spot-on top of a mountain. It wasn't his place to ask questions. He was just following orders. He was paid well to ferry important people and goods around for SIES. Emily was amazed at the beauty of the land as they flew toward the mountains. She was fine with doing a little side trip with such an awesome view. She was still a little upset that Matt wouldn't let her join him on the trip to Germany. The snow-capped mountains glistened in the sunlight. Valleys green with lush plant life occasionally dotted with houses met with the rocky turrets. The Chalet seemed out of place in the pristine anonymity of the mountains. The building was perched on an excavated part of the peak. Its tall, marble columns gave a regal appearance to the main building. Blue roofing adorned the top of the building. Emily watched in wonder as the pilot circled the Chalet preparing to land on a helipad some distance from it. The Chalet had six floors with sculpted windows and silver railings encircling patios on several of the levels. Bushes and trees surrounded the building. There were no cars or signs of life nearby.

"Who owns that beautiful building and how did they ever have it built on top of this mountain?" Emily asked the pilot.

"Probably some rich folks. I never see anyone around. I just drop off stuff in that stone building over there." He pointed to the storage unit near the landing pad.

"Someone must be here if you deliver packages to them." Emily looked around for a path or trail when they landed, but there didn't seem to be one leading to the Chalet.

"Ma'am, I'm going to take these boxes over to the building. Please stay in the copter. It's pretty cold and windy up here. I'll get you home as soon as I'm finished." The pilot put several boxes on a dolly and took them over to the storage unit. While he was doing that Emily snuck out of the helicopter and ran over to the Chalet. The ornate entrance was surrounded by two huge doors with gold doves etched into the surface. She tried the handles, but the doors were locked. She backed up and looked up toward the windows. There were no lights or signs of life. She peaked in through two of the first-floor windows with filmy drapes across them. All she could see were outlines of furniture, no movement. She saw the pilot was returning to the helicopter. She was freezing when she jumped into the passenger seat just before he got back to get another load. When he was finished he lifted off the pad and circled the Chalet. Suddenly the Chalet doors opened, and several people began to walk toward the storage unit. She could see that one of them was Gerald when he looked up and waved to the pilot.

"Stop!! Go back!! Please!" Emily yelled. The pilot looked at her like she was crazy.

"Ma'am, I'm not supposed to bring any visitors here unless ordered to. I can't take you back down there."

"You will take me down there or you will be fired. I'm your boss's wife and he will really be upset if you don't do what I tell you!" Emily sputtered.

"You're Doctor Proctor's wife?! I…I'll let you off right away, Ma'am. Don't freak out." He lowered the helicopter and waited until her feet touched the ground. "Do you want me to wait for you, Ma'am?"

"No, thank you. I'll be all right. Sorry I yelled at you." She hid herself behind the door of the copter until she saw Gerald and the others disappear around the storage building. "You can go. If you see Matt…. Mr. Fornier, tell him I am here, and I will be in touch."

The pilot hesitated to leave her on the top of a treacherous mountain, especially if what she said was true, that she was Proctor's wife. He had never heard anyone say he was married. Despite his misgivings he took off for Geneva. While the helicopter was being refueled for the long trip back to New York, he called Matt Fornier.

Emily headed toward the storage building. The wind tugged at her body and the sight of her Ex tugged at her heart. *What is he doing here? He lied to me and Matt. This is Switzerland, on the top of some God forsaken mountain, not Germany.* She peaked around the side of the building to see if anyone was there. Instead, she gasped when she saw a few steps beyond the back of the unit was a sheer cliff plunging straight down into darkness. She hadn't heard screams. Hopefully, they knew how close the building was to the cliff. She inched against the wall shakily until she saw a door. She cautiously turned the knob and eased into the room. A dim light automatically lit. She closed the door trying not to make any noise. There were boxes stacked along one wall. Next to some of them was a large steel door with a keypad on the wall next to it. It appeared to be an elevator. Emily was cold, hungry and very confused. She was sure it was Gerry with a small group of people that walked from the Chalet to this building. *They must have taken this elevator.* She stared at the keypad not knowing what to do next. Emily sat down on a stack of boxes and held her head in her hands. Stamped on the box where she was sitting there appeared to be a blurred notation. She took a small flashlight from the bottom of her purse and shone it on the lettering. "Indigo-35" was not only on that box but also on several other boxes. She took a chance and punched into the keypad the numbers corresponding to the letters – 46344635. Her hand shook and she held her breath as she punched in the final number. The door opened into a brightly lit elevator with foam padding on the walls. The doors closed and the elevator dropped so fast she had to hang on to the sides in order to keep her balance. She closed her eyes waiting for the elevator car to crash into the bottom. Instead, the car slowed gently and came to a stop, the doors opening. Emily was staring into a huge cave with bright spotlights shining like stars in the rocky ceiling. She blinked her eyes trying to focus. Suspended within tubular structures glistening with an almost liquid-like covering were some sort of spacecraft. The structures were enormous and seemed to be hanging in mid-air. The sound similar to the breathing of a monstrous animal echoed off the walls of the cave. Deep down on what seemed to be the floor there were banks of computers with screens glowing with numbers and other symbols. Some of the computer screens alternated pictures of what seemed to be rooms. She didn't see anyone in around or hear any voices. She noticed she was standing on a metal platform with stairways going up toward the ceiling and other stairways heading down. She decided to take the stairway heading downward telling herself not to look down through the grating. The breathing sounds grew louder as she descended. The stairway ended on another platform much longer than the one near the elevator. Quite some distance away she could see lights. On either side of this platform there were rooms which appeared to be offices and laboratories. Peering cautiously in the glass doors of the rooms she did not see anyone. When she was almost to what appeared to be the end of the runway she looked down through the grating and could see other platforms and rooms suspended below this one. The last two rooms on either side of the platform had shades pulled over the glass doors and windows. She plastered herself against the railing when she heard voices coming from the room near her. The voices were muffled so she could not make out what they were saying. Suddenly the door opened. There was nowhere to go. A tall figure stepped on to the platform as Emily tried to hide behind the door. Another person, slightly shorter than the first stepped out of the room followed by three other people. One of them reached around to close the door and jumped back when he saw Emily cowering there. Her eyes were wide like saucers.

"What the…!." He shouted. The others turned. Staring at her was her Ex, Gerald.

"Gerry!" she shouted.

"Emily! What are you doing here?" Gerry stood there with his mouth open.

Emily saw Wayne who had moved behind the other men.

"Please, gentlemen, go in the other room with them. I will be with you in a few moments." Gerald said calmly. Wayne moved toward Emily, but Gerald stopped him. "Wayne, let me talk to her first." Wayne joined the others as they walked to the other room with shades on the door.

"Gerry, we were so worried about you. Matt and I, we found that you might be in Geneva. We had the police check your house. You told me you were in Germany. Why are you lying? What is going on?" Her voice got louder with each question. Gerry watched her cheeks redden as she became angrier. She was even prettier when she was angry, he thought.

"Ems, you shouldn't be here. I can't explain right now. I am contacting the helicopter pilot. I assume that is how you wound up here. Where is Matt?"

"I don't know where he is. He made me get into the helicopter to be taken back to the States. The pilot had to drop packages off here. That is when I saw you with these other people. Please, please tell me what is going on." Gerry looked at her remembering all the years they spent laughing, loving, raising kids and sharing life's moments together.

"Come with me, Emily." He took her icy hand and led her into the room on the left. Sitting around a table were two women and two men. The three men and Wayne who had been with Gerry in the other room stood against the wall. "This is Emily Proctor, everyone. Emily, these folks are Drs. Erin Coutcher, Henry Stilwacki, and Martin Szechnick. I believe you know Dr. Wayne Romer. Next to him are Colonel Steve Agnue, Colonel Ronald Vandercook and Colonel Daniel Wheeling. These are some of the people who have been working on Indigo-35 project." Wayne stared at the floor.

"What is Indigo-35? I saw that on the boxes in the shed." Emily asked. Several of the people sitting at the table started talking at the same time.

"Settle down!" Gerry shouted. "This is very technical and none of us are able to explain, even if we could. We need to get back to work. Emily, I'll get you back to the helipad." Gerry took her arm firmly and guided her down the platform and up the stairs. When they arrived at the door to the elevator, Emily glanced at Gerry and smiled. He put his arm around her waist, and they rode to the surface without speaking. They stepped out of the building cautiously moving away from the precipitous cliff. Just as they were rounding the side of the building a figure stepped in front of them, frightening Emily. She stepped backward and began to slide over the edge of the cliff. Gerry grabbed for her. He caught one of her arms as she dangled precariously above the abyss. Emily was terrified. She opened her mouth to scream but only a squeak came out.

" Emily, I have you!" Gerry yelled as he tried to reach her other arm. He was holding her outstretched arm in a death grip attempting to pull her up over the edge. Matt ran beside Gerry.

"Emily, put your feet against the face of the rock." Matt yelled. Emily used every bit of strength she had to bend her legs and brace herself against the rock face. Matt reached for her flailing arm almost slipping over the edge himself.

"Hang on, honey! Ems, hang on, we've got you!" Gerry yelled as he and Matt pulled her up and on to the ground. All three laid on the cold ground, exhausted in a post-adrenaline wipe-out. They hugged each other almost smothering Emily between the two men. They laughed and tried to stand. They moved back into the storage building and collapsed on the stacks of boxes. Matt explained how he had gotten up to the top of the mountain. After driving to a small village at the base of Mount Aravis Matt was determined to find a way to get to the top of the mountain. A group of burly residents of the village volunteered to help Matt climb to the top for a price. Only one of the four climbers had managed to get close to the peak. They tethered themselves together with thick ropes and began the climb. The wind had diminished but it was still very cold. Four hours into the climb Matt had to rest. He had always been in excellent shape, but this venture was pushing his sixty-year-old body to the limit. The sound of a helicopter disturbed the silent air. Matt recognized the SIES insignia on the side of the copter and began yelling and waving. The pilot noticed the group and the person waving wildly. Thinking they were stranded and needed help, the pilot hovered over the group and let down a rescue sling. Matt thanked the villagers and strapped himself into the sling. The same pilot that had dropped off Emily pulled Matt into the helicopter. Matt directed the pilot, Tony Ceglio, to take him up to the Chalet. It was Matt who had startled Emily when he approached the storage building. Emily told about her adventure. She recommended the pilot receive a bonus for his extra trips. Gerald knew he would have to reveal at least a part of the journey planned for Indigo-35's mission. He wanted to take Emily with him, but she wasn't trained, and she needed to be home for their kids and grandkids. Gerry told them that three spacecraft along with exploratory rovers were departing soon to bring a space station near Mars. After assessing the terrain and atmosphere on the planet, they hoped to be able to send information back to Earth to determine if Mars could support life. The mission would last several years. The reason for the secrecy was to avoid people panicking or clamoring to volunteer for a visit to the planet. The general public had many years of conflicting reports of aliens entering Earth's atmosphere, the possibility that Armageddon was nearing and all kinds of unverified information. Matt and Emily knew the power of the press. They had seen many instances of news being misinterpreted or embellished. They agreed to keep the project under wraps. Emily was saddened that she and Gerry had bonded once again but could not be together. He was leaving with no real guarantee when and if he would return

CHAPTER VI

LIFT OFF

The crevice near the storage unit was adjacent to the cave containing the Indigo-35 spacecraft, the apparatuses to produce a "universe" between the spacecraft and the containment shells, launching pads, and rockets. The huge opening in the mountain had been created hundreds of years ago when there was a violent eruption of a volcano and an earthquake. The crevice led skyward to a one mile opening in the mountain. Gerry and Wayne had discovered the defect several years before. They devised a plan to explore space light years away after they accidently detected a wormhole. They searched for a location that was remote and could accommodate the equipment, personnel and other tools needed for the project. They needed a place where they could experiment in order to bring the dream of deep space exploration to fruition without being detected. In order to connect the cave to the chiasm they would have to drill small holes in the rock between the two and set small nitroglycerin charges into them. Connecting the charges was extremely dangerous. Each one had to be linked and timed to ignite in sequence. The volatility of nitroglycerin added the risk of premature explosion during handling. When the cascade was completed, one of the technicians was assigned to ignite the initial nitro explosive. The small explosions would crack the connecting wall and rock would fall into the lake below the chiasm. After the explosion, the spaceships and other structures would be moved along a track to the launching pad extending into the chiasm where they could be launched through the volcanic opening.

The Apellonauts had technology to scan through solid objects and gather information. That data was sent back to their planet and other planets in their solar system that were inhabited. The data was converted into language they could understand and evaluate. The Indigo-35 project was of particular interest to them because these primitive beings on Earth had similar characteristics to the primates that had inhabited their planet hundreds of Apello years ago. If they could assist these earthlings in their attempt to journey through a wormhole, they would be able to study them. Now that the nitrogen level on Indigo-35 was the same concentration as Earth's, the ability to keep these earthlings alive and to study them in their laboratories was more feasible. There were other space exploration projects in countries around the globe. None of them, so far, had reached the point where such a bold attempt in space travel was about to be made. The robotic Apellonauts were able to withstand the tumultuous journey through wormholes. Had they retained human-like anatomy it would have been difficult, even impossible, for them to survive the force of negative gravity and turbulence produced when traveling beyond the speed of light. Gerald, Wayne, the scientists and technicians they had recruited to work on the project were confident the shield and man-made universe of exotic energy surrounding the spacecraft would protect them during the journey through time. If they failed, at least they would have left all mission data with the Mars space station and with Madeline back at SIES. Thus, their hard work would not have been entirely in vain.

Emily and Matt arrived back in New York late in the evening. They were exhausted and perplexed by all they had witnessed in the past few days. A space mission hidden in the center of a mountain in Switzerland, almost falling to their death, a project that was surrounded with secrecy and intrigue and an unsettled feeling that they were not being told the truth preyed on their minds. Emily needed to put together a story that would be believable, not incite a panic and advance her position in the Times. She avoided telling how she obtained the information about an expansion of the Mars exploration. The general public was aware that there had been a Bill passed by Congress to support the construction of a space station and also research into a substance that would protect plant life and soil from chemicals used in pesticides. She wrote about the facts and gently approached the controversial subject of climate change. Her boss was excited when he read her draft of the article. She wanted to include the names of Gerry and Wayne and the sacrifice they were making. She and Matt honored their request not to mention SIES or their names. Matt returned to SIES and began an intensive tracking of expenses surrounding the Indigo-35 project, travel vouchers and anything else he could dig up about why this project was full of secrets. He contacted some of the technicians that had worked in the SIES lab but none of them had much to add to what Gerry had told him.

Wednesday, December 11, 2014. Mars and the Earth were only in an elliptical path that could accommodate a spacecraft's ability to reach Mars in twenty-six months. Several attempts of manned spacecraft had been made in 2012 without success. The SIES launch pad, spacecraft in their processing tubes, radiological equipment to inject the exotic mass "universe" into the capsules surrounding the spaceships, rocket launchers were moved into place within the cave and adjacent to the rock chiasm. The astronauts that would pilot the craft, Erin and most of her team plus several scientific and aerospace experts, Gerald and Wayne prepared to enter the spacecrafts after the wall was destroyed between the cave and the chiasm. Erin had decided to join the crew. She felt the information they would be sending back to Earth would be the greater contribution to saving the planet than her staying behind. Each of the crew were dressed in pressurized suits built to withstand the G-force as the ships rocketed through the atmosphere. Gerald signaled the operator manning a bank of computers that would control the ignition of the explosives. Ten-nine-eight-seven……..three-two-one, Gerald's arm rose in the air. The sound of each explosion was deafening. The rock wall turned to powder as each section imploded and the debris fell into the lake below. The final nitro capsule was detonated, and the cave expanded into the chiasm. The opening into the sky high above the floor of the cave looked small from where the crew stood. The platform, launch pad and space craft were moved into place. The crew entered their assigned spacecraft and belted themselves into the cushioned seats. The pilots of each ship flipped the buttons to prepare the launch rockets filled with liquid Oxygen to begin pressurizing. The booster rockets would launch each ship sequentially as they broke through the stratosphere. The rockets burned off as the spaceships entered the Exosphere. Each crew member had been exposed to the G-forces during training. As the spacecraft were propelled through the seven layers of Earth's atmosphere they felt those forces in real time. The monitor tracking their vital signs (B/P, pulse, respiration, oxygen levels) indicated the crew was tolerating the immense pressure, which pressed them deep into their seats. Once the ships had reached over seventy-five miles into the atmosphere, positioning rockets on the sides and back of the huge spacecraft aimed them toward Mars. The journey to that planet would take anywhere from one hundred to two-hundred and fifty days. Hypergolic propellants, which ignite on contact, were used to maneuver the spacecraft The scientists had found this to be the best type of propellant as it does not require an ignition source. It ignites spontaneously on contact. The artificial universe and shield would be formed when the ships arrived near Mars and the space station was launched into orbit around the planet. The space station had been placed in the mother ship which had the largest aft compartment. Gerald and his pilot, Colonel Ronald Vandercook, marveled at the colors of stars and the endless depth of the galaxies their craft was streaming through. Asteroids and eerie green and blue transparent rivers of gases were avoided by Ron's skilled mastery of the controls. Wayne's ship was piloted by Colonel Steve Ague. He had made several trips to space stations and to repair instruments on satellites. He had a quirky sense of humor which took Wayne a while to get used to. The third ship was piloted by Colonel Daniel Wheeling. Henry and Martin accompanied him on this ship. Erin was assigned to Gerald's ship. Each of the spaceships had four additional highly trained technicians that had experience with aerospace travel and had been selected from the technicians who worked at the SIES lab. There was one of the Captain robots assigned to each of the ships. Henry and Martin were not surprised that 0-10 joined them on Indigo-M2, R.D. Quincy. Weightlessness was a little disorienting at first even though all of the crew members had experienced the phenomenon in simulation training capsules. Objects that were not housed in fixed holders wandered around the bunk, kitchen, and research areas of the ship. To prevent hazards, loose objects were strictly forbidden in the cockpit. Henry, entranced by space gases and debris, sometimes forgot the rule, releasing instruments and his favorite snack—mellochips—to float away (small round pieces of protein and dehydrated banana and cranberries). Gerald and Ron reprimanded him but secretly laughed at his incoordination.

Madeline had been torn between her passion for risk taking and her family. The team understood; it was a difficult decision for her, as for all of them. Gerald trusted her to keep the actual mission a secret until they had arrived safely and explored Indigo-35. Communication would only be possible if they could reverse a wormhole so that portals surrounded by the same substance used in the shields to contain universes with exotic mass had similar qualities. These would attach themselves to the space station. Madeline was set up in a special office at SIES NY where only she would receive the transmissions sent to the space station. She was content to be chosen to manage this critical part of the mission and still be there for her family. Photographs on specially designed computer chips could be downloaded into a computer designed to project images light years away. She would follow the directions of the project managers if there should be loss of communications or worse.

Day 38, January 25, 2015. Henry was convinced that the blue and green gaseous streams that appeared and disappeared throughout their journey were chemical substances not available on earth. He was sure they were used by alien beings to perform observation and extraction of information from planets, galaxies and other space objects outside of their own galaxy. Over the past 38 days of their journey the crew of each spacecraft had settled into comfortable routines performing experiments, researching space gases and particles, making repairs and adjustments outside and inside the ships and generally getting along with each other. Though there were times when each of the crew became anxious, discouraged or longing for their friends and families they became comfortable sharing these concerns and accepting encouragement and feedback. Henry and Martin had devised a way to extract samples from the streams with a vacuum system that was attached to the port and starboard sides of the spacecraft. It was used to pull air into the ship, analyze the composition of the sample and return it to the surrounding universe. The only problem was in order to extract from a specific area in a short period of time that the stream was present, one of the crew would need to uncouple the vacuum devise and aim it directly at the stream. Martin volunteered to perform the manual portion outside of the ship. He would be tethered to the ship. Henry would perform the analysis inside the ship on the computer. He would have barely fifteen minutes to extract whatever information he visualized not knowing how the stream would react if it was controlled by an intelligent being as he suspected. Martin suited up, tested his communication system, attached the tether and the lifeline that supplied oxygen to his helmet, tested the various visualization visors inside the faceplate of his helmet. There were four visors: blue, red, yellow and clear. Henry and he had been able to visualize the green streams using clear or yellow visors. Since there had also been a few blue streams, the other visors could be flipped over the face of the helmet to visualize them should they appear. They had found the streams usually appeared late in the day on and off for about an hour. Each sighting had lasted less than ten seconds. Martin would have to disengage the vacuum cannister from the ship and be ready to extract immediately upon visualization. If the extraction were successful, Henry would receive an audible so he could rapidly perform an analysis. Then Martin would release the stream back into the surrounding universe, reconnect the device and return into the ship. The risk was heightened beyond the usual one carried with extravehicular activity (EVA) because they did not know what kind of gases they were nor who or what controlled them.

Martin made the sign of the cross as he entered the chamber that led to the exit hatch. The panorama outside the ship was mesmerizing. Earth was not clearly visible, stars and other small asteroids flashed by the ship. The colors were not like any he had seen on Earth. Since he had manned several other space missions and had performed some EVA while he was at NASA, he limited his gaze of the endlessness of space and used the handles on the sides of the ship to move to the port side where the canister was located. From the toolbelt attached to his spacesuit he withdrew a battery powered tool to open the clamps holding the canister. It would take a good amount of dexterity to hang on to the canister after it was unclamped. The atmosphere would grab hold of it and whisk it away if he couldn't attach the hook and tether to hold on to it at the same time he replaced the power tool onto his belt. Henry was watching for any sign of the streams to appear on the radar inside the ship. Just as Martin had gotten the canister secured, almost slipping away from the ship when he had to let go of the handles, Henry shouted "Martin, to your left heading from the front of the ship! There is a large, green stream." Martin flipped down the yellow visor and turned to his left. The stream unsulated and made a drum-like sound similar to a heartbeat. Even with his helmet protecting his ears the sound pounded against his eardrums. He aimed the nose of the cannister toward the mass that now was surrounding him. He pushed the trigger to begin extracting some of the gases.

"God, Henry! It's full of sparkling particles—they're hitting my faceplate, burning through my suit! The noise... I can't stand it!" Martin screamed.

"Marty, ABORT!! ABORT! Get back in the ship! Marty…. can you hear me?" Henry yelled to two of the crew that were in the living quarters. "I need help! Martin is being attacked…. Marty?? Come in Martin! Come in Martin!" A crewman named Jack hurried to the dressing area and he quickly jammed his body into the pressurized suit, hooked up tethers and life support and exited the ship. Henry propelled himself into the cockpit, screaming that Martin was under attack. Colonel Wheeling had been skeptical about Henry and Martin's request to perform the extraction of an unknown substance and also of Martin performing an EVA to do it. He had given in, against his better judgement.

"If he is on the port side, I can slowly jettison one of the rockets that will rotate the ship to the right. Hopefully, Jack can get to him when we pull away from this thing." The Colonel ordered Henry to sit.

"I have to analyze the gas Martin collected, and someone needs to vent the canister—now! We don't know what it will do attached to the ship!" Henry was sweating. Dan Wheeling shoed him away while he notified Jack who was hanging on to the ship watching Martin dissolve into the gaseous green mass. He couldn't get near him, or he would be absorbed by the stuff. He was sick, feeling helpless. He heard Dan tell him that he was going to try to rotate the ship away from the stream and that Jack needed to try and rescue Martin, release the gas from the canister and attach it back onto the ship.

"Colonel... there's hardly anything left of Dr. Szechnick. That thing... it dissolved him!" Jack's voice shook. Then, suddenly, the stream vanished, the pounding sound stopped as the ship turned slowly to the right. Very cautiously, Jack inched towards the spot where the cannister hung by the clamp Martin had attached. There was no sign of Martin nor the "thing". Jack quickly reversed the vacuum and blew out the contents. The only thing that he could see leave the mouth of the cannister were tiny sparkling particles that hovered for a few seconds and then disappeared into the darkness. He looked out into space and reported that he saw nothing…no Martin. He re-attached the vacuum cannister to the ship and dejectedly returned inside the compression chamber. After removing his space suit and helmet, he floated into the lab where Henry was staring at the computer. Tears were streaming down his face as he sat strapped to his chair. Henry patted Jack on his shoulder and Jack floated into the cockpit to report to Colonel Wheeling.

"Sir, I have never seen anything like that! It was swirling around Marty. It…it had these flashing things swirling around him…they sparkled like diamonds. The noise was drumming…really loud. I could hear it through my helmet. It had a rhythm like a heartbeat. I…I couldn't do anything. I'm so sorry, Sir." Jack couldn't get the image of Martin being swallowed by that awful green stream of …whatever it was.

"Jack, go to your quarters and rest. I know you did your best. We don't know what that was and how it could make a person disappear. Maybe Dr. Stilwacki can learn something from the analyzer when he examines some of the "gas" remaining in the container." Dan nodded to Jack who was looking pale and somber.

"Yes, Sir." Jack moved slowly toward the bunk area. He passed Henry who was feverishly making notations as he peered at the computer screen. "Henry…anything yet?"

Henry turned and gazed at Jack. His face was flushed and the skin around his eyes was puffy and red. "I am sick about talking him into that EVA. This stream…look at this, Jack."

Jack moved over to the computer and watched as Henry sifted through images of Martin's extracting the cannister and pointing it at the green stream. When it appeared, he had flipped the switch to suction some of the stream was sucked into the cannister. Suddenly, the stream began to take on a form. The outline resembled the silhouette of a human, but the head was very large for what appeared to be a body with several appendages. Long finger-like tentacles grabbed hold of Martin and pulled him into the "body". Tiny sparkling particles moved out of the form as it dissolved along with Martin. The stream undulated and moved away from the spacecraft. It zoomed into the darkness of space.

"Holy mackerel! Was there a…body…a form in that stream? It pulled Martin into its …I can't believe it! It looked alive!" Jack's eyes were as big as saucers. They were glued to the screen.

"The analyzer wasn't able to identify any of the chemicals making up the phenomenon except Nitrogen and one that we noticed in the SIES laboratory. PP was its name given to the substance, Polyprotanium phosphate seems to bond with Nitrogen and form a gas, a solid or a liquid depending on the molecular weight and the atmosphere that surrounds it. Those are the same components identified in the portion of a stream that was captured in the lab." Henry returned to his notes. He just had to stop thinking about Marty. There seemed to be nothing to explain what had happened. Henry had informed the other spacecraft crews of the incident. Erin was shocked and utterly devastated about Martin's disappearance. Henry gave her a few details about the stream and how it had appeared to morph into a form and absorb his friend. She notified her crew and pilot to be on the lookout for a green or blue stream that appeared and disappeared. The streams I-18 team had observed had been as large as a highway. Henry told her this stream was narrower and there was an extremely loud sound emitted from it. Erin's scientific brain throbbed as she internalized and postulated the information trying to equate it with the research she knew about life from other planets. Years of research and theories regarding alien beings had been documented but not proven. No monsters with horns and tentacles, ray guns and laser weaponry had been captured or unearthed. Perhaps this was a breakthrough. They now had pictures of a form attacking a human. Had they made a discovery that scientists had researched for decades? The sacrifice of anyone was always disheartening. Martin's life had been sacrificed. In doing so, he had given support for a long-standing hypothesis. There were other life forms. They had the photos to prove it. Jack had not seen the form as he was focused on Martin melting into the stream.

The portion of the stream that was trapped in the cannister and being analyzed sent communication into space to the alien ships posted in Earth's atmosphere, space observation and retaliatory ships near Mars and to the Apellonaut's planet SIES had named Indigo-35.

A small alien transportation ship carried the sleeping astronaut, Martin, to one of the larger observation ships. It eased into an opening at the front of the larger ship. That ship sent out radiological signals until it located a wormhole and was transported forty-five light years to a landing surface in the newly built city above ground on Indigo-35. Giant tubes housed transportation capsules that moved the Apellonauts to destinations in the city or to elevators leading to underground locations. Martin slept.

Day 108, April 25, 2015; The three ships had not encountered another stream. Ship M-2, R.D. Quincy, had also been notified of Martin's disappearance. Erin sent a message to Madeline about Marty. She was devastated. Even though she teased him and Henry incessantly she had a high regard for their intelligence and commitment. Wayne and Gerald reviewed the images of Martin's EVA and the strange movements and formations of the stream. Wayne was not as enthusiastic about the theory of this stream morphing into an alien form. There was a form, he agreed, but not a life form. He surmised it looked more like an electrical field concentrated withing the actual gaseous material of the stream. The Polyprotanium Phosphate present in the sample was gathered from the crystal particles floating in the gas. Nitrogen was the only element they could identify in the gaseous material. They could find no other elements that earthlings knew about. The green coloring of the stream disappeared when sucked into the cannister. Perhaps the stream depended on another element, gas, or particle in space in order to display a color. With the assistance of an electron microscope, some of the particles extracted from the cannister were able to be viewed. Each particle was magnified one-hundred times. The cell bodies had a protein membrane and tiny filaments extending from the membrane. Some of the particles were a greenish color, others were blue. The inside of the cells were composed of a liquid substance that neither the analyzer nor the scientists could identify. No DNA or RNA patterns that were recognizable to the scientists existed. The linear string of atoms within the liquid substance was unidentifiable. There were no nuclei as are present in our living cells. The few similarities of the particles to cells in living beings gave even more clarity to the hypothesis of alien life forms. Henry knew it was a wild supposition, but he wondered if Martin, and perhaps other interesting matter were transported rather than "eaten" by something or from being in the stream. He and Martin were both certain that earthlings were not the only life forms in the Universe. Too many instances and sightings that could not be explained had been documented. Some extraterrestrial observations were reported hundreds of years ago. Henry knew he was needed during the rest of the journey, especially now that Martin was not available. He pushed the crazy thought of exposing himself to the stream held in the cannister to see if the same fate would befall him.

That is not an option. Just eliminate that insane thought! Henry glanced around the cabin. He hoped 0-10 couldn't read his thoughts. He really did not see why any of the Captains would be included in the mission.

Day 258, August 21, 2015. Mars dangled in space, a rose-colored sphere beckoning the weary crews of the Indigo spaceships to be swallowed into its violent dust storms, bottomless crevices and monstrous mountains. The plan was to eject the space station, dock the spacecraft and refresh themselves before locating the wormhole for the final trip to Indigo-35 (Apello). The scientists and technicians analyzed and categorized the information sent to the space station from the rovers that had been placed on Mars during past missions. Thousands of photographs of the planet, data from soil and other samples from the surface and air had been collected. Human exploration of the planet was not planned until 2025. If successful a space shuttle carrying volunteers from several walks of life, astronauts and scientists was being proposed. Dr. Gerald Proctor hoped that he would only have aged five years by the time they reached Indigo-35. If the planet were inhabitable and if there were an advanced species already living there, perhaps they could join forces for a transport back to Mars when that Mars mission occurred. Lots of "ifs". The old, risk-averse Gerald would never have dreamed he'd be in a space station near Mars preparing to travel through a wormhole to live on a planet five light years away. There was a reason he had insisted on taking three of the Captains, one on each ship. He hadn't shared it with Wayne or any other of the crew. Those robots had been designed for a far more global reason than to watch over a bunch of technicians. In a secret testing site near SIES Colorado, simulations of the terrain, atmosphere and climate of Mars had been established a couple of years before Gerald had risen to CEO of SIES. SIES was part of the conglomerate of financiers who privately were planning a mission to inhabit Mars. Gerald became fascinated with this arm of the organization. His brilliant mind drew plans for humans altered by artificial intelligence methods into obedient robots that could be programmed to follow commands and a job description. He had eliminated emotion from their data bases. They did not need oxygen or a particular atmospheric condition to survive. They would be able to withstand the extreme cold temperatures and thin Carbon Dioxide atmosphere. Their physical strength was ten times that of a champion wrestler and their bodies bullet, laser and fireproof. As his compulsion for extending the Mars mission to remote planets light years from earth grew his respect and discernment for the value of human lives diminished. He never thought that AI could become so developed that it could counter its programmed decision making if it were for its own benefit, a computerized narcissism.

Erin was assigned the task that Martin had once performed. She was glued to the computer to watch for any signs of the wormhole or a visit from the stream. The cameras attached to the space station and to the spaceships were extremely sensitive. They could pick up images not noticeable to the naked eye. The definition of images could be viewed three dimensionally and detail remained pristine when images were examined microscopically. Jack recovered from the aborted EVA except for the harrowing images of the stream absorbing Martin. Erin's and Gerald's focus appeared to have moved from studying the portion of the stream remaining in the cannister attached to the ship to information from Mars and finding a wormhole. Jack had been in the Navy since he graduated from college with an aerospace engineering degree. His goal to fly missions to the moon and planets was fulfilled in 1996 when he accompanied two other NASA pilots on the third mission to the moon. When he saw that the analysis of the cannister contents was diverted once they expelled the space station, he made plans to detach the cannister and send it tumbling through space. He had lost sleep just knowing that hideous monster was still attached to the ship. Dreams of the entire crew including himself being eaten by the hitchhiker woke him in a sweat and trembling. He covered his fear well while he worked on the space station.

There was a great amount of work being done on the space station to make sure its orbit was intact around Mars and that all systems were functioning flawlessly. Six men and two women would remain on the space station for eighteen months gathering information from the planet in preparation for the first astronauts to plant feet on Mars in 2025. If they survived the planet's atmosphere and rugged terrain their job would be to build structures, greenhouses and a base camp for the future inhabitants.

Gerald would be inhabiting another planet when the Mars mission progressed. He needed to see if a prototype of a human could survive well before 2025. While Erin intently perused the images in space surrounding the parked space station Gerald programmed 0-10 to perform exploration of Mars, construction of a pod with properties similar to the pod in which the Captains resided in the SIES laboratory. Gerald programmed the robot's organs to require the same atmospheric conditions that real humans needed to survive on earth. If 0-10's spacesuit and helmet would allow him to erect the pod and create an environment within it to live, Gerald would be heralded as a hero, and he would have information to assist him and the other crew members to survive on Indigo-35. One very important feature that humans would have to deal with on missions would be emotions. Fear, fatigue, excitement, hope – 0-10 and the other robots did not have these. These innate human qualities help human beings to proceed with caution, overcome loneliness and persist with courage. In his quest for recognition and creation of a perfect specimen, Gerald had forgotten how this critical difference was paramount in the processes of discovery and perception.

CHAPTER VII

ALIENS?

The mountains on the "Red Planet" were mainly composed of iron oxide. The average temperature was -52 degrees F, compared to Earth's Antarctica -57 degrees F. It could vary from 60°F to -225°F. There were raging dust storms and the atmosphere was very thin. A day was 24.37 hours, but a year was 687 days. Gravity was 62% lower than Earth's; thus, a person weighing one hundred pounds on Earth would weigh only 38 pounds on Mars. Microgravity, which astronauts experience in space and would live with on Mars, can cause muscle wasting, hypertension, eyesight problems and problems with proprioception. Many studies and proposals to send humans to Mars had been presented since 1970. The trajectory of the planet and Earth would have to sync in order to reach Mars in nine months. Several of the obstacles astronauts would face during the mission and the time spent exploring the planet were the light gravity, isolation, hostile terrain and climate, radiation and separation from their fellow Earthlings. Another concern was how to have enough fuel to return to Earth after living on the planet for one to three years. One option was to send an unmanned ship that would produce fuel by extracting methane and oxygen from the CO2 in the air (similar to a gaslight) and from products existing on the planet. That fuel could be used in the manned spacecraft for a return flight. Gerald and Wayne, along with other passionate scientists had been discouraged by the roller coaster of interest in funding a Mars mission based on the political mindset of various administrations. Gerald persisted in his plans to utilize Mars as a base for his goal to travel to Indigo-35 and other planets in its galaxy. Wayne focused on developing rovers, spacecraft surface agents and the materials for building structures to be delivered and constructed on Mars. He did not know that Gerald was going to use his Captain robots as experimental inhabitants of the planets to improve the chances of humans living on them. Gerald and Wayne were more convinced there were other life forms in the universe since they had observed the stream and its ability to make decisions and possibly transport a human by an unusual osmotic process absorbing its body.

The two Mars rovers were outfitted with the most advanced shielding, computerized equipment and adaptations to extract samples and analyze them upon retrieval. They could explore the planet driven by a pilot or be remotely controlled from the spacecraft or pods constructed as living quarters, greenhouses and laboratories by the astronauts. The rovers would be transported by a booster rocket attached to the underside of the spider-like vehicles. Gerald planned to have 0-10 make the journey. He knew he would *be* questioned about the addition of a semi-human artificial intelligence sent to a planet to establish a base camp alone. He rationalized that the robot would be collecting valuable information without risking actual human lives. Since he had been programmed with human organs the physical stresses of the planet's terrain, the flight and the atmosphere could be monitored. When the rover, booster and fuel spacecraft were ready to be launched on day 325 of their mission, Gerald shared his plan to send 0-10 to Mars. Reluctantly, Wayne and the other crew members agreed. 0-10 was outfitted with a spacesuit and helmet that had been tested for its competency to withstand the frigid temperature, deliver breathable air to the lungs and to monitor vital signs of the person (or specimen) wearing the gear. Since the Captain robots had no emotions 0-10 obeyed the commands programmed for the mission without hesitancy, questioning or fear.

Beneath the enormous, iron rich mountains on the red planet there had been life forms millions of years ago when there was water on the planet. Microscopic pedeculites, one-celled organisms with hair-like filaments covering the body, had adapted to the fierce temperature changes, violent storms and thin atmosphere by a process known as osmotic selection. The outer surface of the cell utilized the filaments to extract and filter gases, chemicals and other elements needed for the organism to survive. As the planet gradually changed its orbit one million Mars years ago, it moved closer to the sun at one point. The course became more elliptical, thus causing water to dry up and vast differences in temperature to occur. The pedeculites structure adapted to these radical changes by burrowing deep beneath the mountains, using CO_2 and nitrogen for cell respiration and eliminating the design of the cells' nuclei DNA. Because of this the cells multiplied creating a life-form ten feet tall, cylindrical and highly intelligent. These early Martians never left the cave cities in the mountains. Adventurous prospectors tunneled their way to the surface only to freeze or burn in the extreme temperatures. The filaments became arms with long sharp fingers attached. The "head" was an expanded portion of the cylinder with large infrared eyes able to penetrate complete darkness.

The "mouth" was a tube that could extract fossils of their former selves from the rock for nutrition. Communication was performed by telepathic messages sent from the immense "brain" in their heads. Their brain was much different than the earthling brain. It developed from a series of particles charged with eletro-magnetic ions very similar to the "brains" of computers. The Martian brains were able to perform highly advanced mathematical calculations in seconds, determine surface changes in the terrain and atmosphere of the planet from their vantage point underground and catalogue and extract enormous amounts of information in seconds. There were no areas of their brains specific for emotions. Their actions and functions were purely based on analysis of the information and connections pre-determined to react to the result of the analysis. They reproduced via a similar process. Calculations of needs for gathering, mining, or defense prompted an individual Martian to divide into one or more beings depending on the results of the calculations. The civilization developed without the need for arguments, aggression or war. Healthy debate was encouraged because it enhanced the intelligence of the Martian and produced equations within the brain to speed up processes of decision making.

0-10 arrived on Mars without any major problems. The amount of time from the rocket launch at the space station to landing on Mars was two days and thirty-four minutes. Recordings of 0-10's vital signs and muscular activity during the flight were acceptable. An EEG (electroencephalogram), used to monitor a human astronaut, would have been of little use since the robot's "brain" was a computer. The space module contained inflatable buildings made of a material that could withstand any violent storms, thin atmospheric conditions and low gravity. 0-10 had been instructed to suit up, release the rover from the module, begin to produce fuel from methane and CO2, inflate and secure three of the compact buildings and begin to extract oxygen from the atmospheric CO2 placing 50% of it in holding tanks and the other 50% into Hydrogen filled tanks to combine with the hydrogen to make water. Since sleep was not needed by Captain robots he could complete his tasks without a rest period. Robots did not need to eat. An implant under the human skin provided nourishment for the human organs. It could be refilled by 0-10 from ampules stored within the laboratory building.

The Martians detected activity on the surface above them. It was different from the usual storms, asteroid collisions and atmospheric conditions tracked routinely. Visual imprints of the space module, inflated buildings, 0-10 and the new rover were sent to the observation equipment underground. Since there had been unmanned rovers on Mars in the past this new one was not cause for review. Attempts by prior rovers to establish pods or buildings in the past had not been successful. 0-10 was a new object appearing on the imprint screen. It was identified as an alien, part human and part artificial intelligence. There had been little interest in exploring these beings from earth who wandered about the Mar's atmosphere in pre-historic ships and sending clumsy transport vehicles to the surface grabbing samples from the soil, mountains and air. The Martians' brains devised a plan to extract 0-10 from the surface and bring it to their underground dwelling for study and research. Their technology could produce a stream that could penetrate the surface without harm to the inhabitants. It had the ability to disorganize the cells of any intruder, alive or otherwise, absorb those cells or matter into particulate transport mobilizers in the stream and take them to a pre-determined site. The same process had been used to take

Martin from his tethered EVA outside M-1 to a laboratory aboard an Apellonaut's spaceship. 0-10 sent continuous information back to the scientists and crew of the Indigo-35 mission. It was encouraging that the human portion of the robot was surviving the rigors of the planet. Consideration for humans' need for rest and other unforeseen effects of extraterrestrial living would have to be factored into the information received from 0-10 and the other Captain robots in order to evaluate the risks for the planned mission to Mars by humans in 2025.

0-10's computer detected an unusual energy disturbance on his tenth day on Mars. His programs could not identify the cause or imprint of the event. It was displayed on the monitors in the space station as static electricity. That was impossible as far away from the earth as the Mars space station was roaming above the atmosphere of the planet. Henry, Wayne, Erin and several of the other scientists observing 0-10 attempted numerous blocking techniques in order to be able to clear the static to no avail. 0-10 observed a transparent green stream entering the laboratory building. There were no additional commands or instructions about the intrusion. 0-10 continued to perform the activities sent to him from the space station. The human parts of the robot began to heat up and be absorbed by the transport particles in the stream. The space station scientists could see rapid temperature spikes and tachycardia off the charts coming on the monitor of 0-10's heart and regulatory system. Inter-planetary communication developed as alien beings specialized their computerized systems. These advanced AI systems could translate any incoming data from the format of another alien society to their own language. The Martians had received information from several other planets' observation satellites that a live form of an earthling had been transported to Apellonauts' laboratories for study. When 0-10 arrived in the underground laboratory of the Martians the two alien societies automatically shared their research with each other and several aliens of other planets in the Universe. In the past there was little interest in earthlings. Recent events stimulated their curiosity as there seemed to be more than just the run of the mill earthling exploring distant space. This one roaming around on the surface of their planet appeared to have some of the qualities the Martians possessed as well as those of inhabitants of other planets.

Emily couldn't stop thinking about her Ex-husband. News from Europe reported sightings of UFO's near a mountain range several miles from Geneva Switzerland. These appeared to be missiles rising into the atmosphere from an undisclosed position, unlike other sightings reporting hovering objects in the atmosphere rather than exiting. There were several of these "missiles", each of three fiery trails seen disappearing into space after thirty minutes. Seismic fluctuations at weather stations in the region reported earthquake activity in the vicinity of the mountain range one hour prior to sighting of the first UFO was reported. The village below Mount Aravis had no record of an earthquake or other disturbance at that time. No launcher debris was reported within a one-hundred-mile radius as would have been seen had it been a rocket or ship from Earth. When the report came over the wire of the unusual sightings Emily smiled. Her reporter's gut wanted more than anything to write what she had experienced at Chaine D' Aravis but she had promised Gerald she would not tell anyone. Seeing him had unearthed so many old feelings she had buried. Looking into his handsome face, seeing his passion for this adventure, and the warmth of his touch helped her to understand how monumental this mission was. Visions of the spacecraft, the technology and vast amount of planning and research that it had to have taken to put this together, she began to understand why Gerald had changed and his tireless commitment to see it through. She worried about the huge risk he and the others were taking for the cause of space exploration. She needed to be part of it.

Emily went to her boss. "Mr. Churney, I have a request." He chewed on his cigar and did not look up from the papers on his desk. "Bill, I need to follow this story about sightings of UFO's near Geneva.

He looked at her, still mouthing the moist cigar, "Emily, didn't you get enough skiing when you were there last month?" he snarled but with a half grin.

"This isn't a vacation. You know I have followed SIES for years…and…I think the company may have something to do with those sightings. They have been involved in pushing for funding of a chemical that could not only save plant life and soil but also could be used to protect spacecraft traveling at tremendous speeds. You know I did an article on Senator Eddleman's Bill to fund a SIES project long term. I have a hunch that might be the project." Emily sat in the chair in front of his desk.

"Hmmm… a hunch, eh? You know it's risky following hunches. I'll agree to your working on this. The public loves sci-fi stuff. Do you have any reliable contacts at SIES? If what you think is true the company is going to gag this for sure, especially if it risks lives."

"I might have contact with one of the scientific technicians who used to work in the laboratory. It was very sudden the company closed the lab that was working on that substance for plants. I haven't heard any ripples on the street as to why it was closed. What happened to the research and was the project a success? I promise I will stay in the cheapest hotel when I go to Switzerland to get more info. I won't ski." Emily smiled her most alluring smile. Bill Churney had been married three unsuccessful times, but he still appreciated a beautiful lady like Emily. She was smart too.

"Okay, set everything up with communications and keep me up to date…… and, Ems, be careful. That is a big company, and they might get pissed if they know the press is snooping around." Bill smushed out his cigar and leaned back in his chair as he watched Emily stand and leave the room.

Only a few people besides Gerald had called her Ems. It gave her heart a little flutter. "I'll be careful. I can take care of myself. Not to worry. Thanks, Bill. You won't regret it." She closed the door softly. Bill sighed and went back to his paperwork.

◄ ◄ ✖ ► ►

Martin tried to focus. A bright light pierced his vision. He couldn't move his arms or legs. He realized he was no longer in his space suit. His body felt like it was covered with a filmy material. The last thing he remembered was doing something with tools outside the spacecraft. Maybe he was in the medical section of the space station. What had happened to him out there? Why couldn't he move? Suddenly, there were two strange looking "things" hovering over him wearing the weirdest space helmets he had ever seen covering their heads. The helmets had several large "eyes" and some type of antenna sprouting from the top. The "eyes" glowed with different colors. Martin tried to speak. His throat was extremely dry. The words came out as a whisper.

"Hey guys, what happened to me? Where did you get those crazy helmets? Why do you have me strapped down?" Martin tried once more to move his limbs – nothing, not even a sensation. "Oh, God, am I paralyzed?!" his heart was pounding. Neither person hovering over him answered. As his eyes regained focus, he looked around the room. Nothing looked familiar. There were glowing panels with large screens picturing space three dimensionally Images of planets, stars, suns, asteroids sped by on the screens. A strange pulsation, low and drum-like echoed throughout the room. He could not feel any surface supporting his body. It was as if he was suspended. Then he saw the bodies of the two attendants. They were long and cylindrical. Multiple appendages with long glowing "fingers" exited the bodies. The "fingers" were touching him, attaching wires, searching his body. He could see them touching him but could feel nothing. He didn't feel warm or cold. Sweat began to run down the sides of his face. He wanted to scream, to get out of wherever he was. Fear clutched at his throat as one of the "hands" touched his temples and he drifted into a dark tunnel of sleep.

0-10 was in a similar room as Martin. He, too, was not able to move. His brain still was imprinted with the last instructions from the space station.

Erect three Pods near the E2372 Mountain Range. Two labs and one living quarters.
Plant seeds in the mixture of Martian soil and chemicals in the laboratory pod. Water them and document the time and amount of all the components.

That was the last order. 0-10 tried to get up to go to the lab pod and follow the instructions, but no part of him responded. Something with glowing beams passed back and forth over his body. He received a command into his computer brain.

What are you called?

0-10 answered telepathically. "I am Captain 0-10. I will mix the soil, plant and water."

What is your mission?

"Release rovers. Collect samples. Build Pods. Grow food. Prepare fuel. Mix soil. Plant seeds. Water them." 0-10 listed his commands.

Are you an earthling?

"I come from earth. I am 0-10. I am a robot."

You have human skin and organs. You are a human.

"I am a robot. I have human skin and organs for study. I will mix the soil, plant and water."

Who made you?

"I am Captain 0-10. I am with SIES mission Indigo-35. I will mix the soil, plant and water."

The Martians sent the information to the Apellonauts. They had communicated they were studying a being that appeared to be human. The being had come from an Earth spaceship. They copied the language transmission from 0-10 and adjusted their telepathic speech module to speak in the specimens' language.

"Are you a robot?" they asked Martin. The voice was deep and mechanical. It sounded like a computer voice.

Martin realized he was aboard an alien ship or on a planet, and these were the real thing. "I…. I am not a robot. I am a human from Earth. I am an astronaut and a scientist." He stammered.

"Why is a robot with human parts exploring Mars?" the voice asked. Martin didn't understand at first. Then he remembered that Dr. Proctor had brought along on the spaceships three of his lab Captain robots.

Maybe he sent one on a test mission to Mars while the crews were preparing to leave the space station to head toward Indigo-35.

"We are Apellonauts from Apello. It is a planet five light years from your Earth. Earthlings are primitive beings. Earthlings do not have the ability to travel through negative gravity in a wormhole." There was no emotion in the voice. It was just reporting observations. Martin tried to hide his terror. The Apellonauts and Martians did not experience emotions. *"You may get up and stand on your appendages. We know that Earthlings eat particles called "food". Do you want some "food"?"*

Martin started to feel his body. He stood from being suspended. He had a silvery jump suit covering his body. It was soft and extremely comfortable. Even the chronic arthritic aches in his shoulders were gone. It was a strange feeling. The aliens floated toward a panel in the wall. *"Come. Food."* The voice said as the aliens (Apellonauts) floated through the panel. Martin followed, feeling hesitant but when he reached the panel he floated through it into a softly lit room. There was a cushiony couch and a small table in the middle of the room. He felt lightheaded and less frightened. The aliens motioned to him to sit on the couch. He sat into a downy, soft, velvety fabric that seemed to hug his body, keeping him from floating around the room. A plate containing what appeared to be a large steak, baked potatoes and slender asparagus; a cup of coffee, a glass of clear water, utensils and a linen napkin appeared on the table covered with a clear dome. One of the aliens pointed to the meal. The voice said, *"You can eat through the covering. It will keep the "food" on the plate. Just put one of your appendages into the dome. It will part for you as you take the food.* Martin was starved. He was amazed that he could move his hand in and out of what appeared to be a solid covering. He looked around the room and saw that computer screens had images of his internal organs, his heart rate, his food entering his mouth, esophagus and the rest of his gastro-intestinal track.

They're able to see right into my body! I must be dreaming. This isn't real! But he could taste the delicious food, cooked to perfection. The coffee was the better than he ever had on Earth. The aliens floated around the room and in and out of the mysterious panel. When one of them passed by him the drumming sound grew louder. It wasn't irritating. In fact, it seemed to soothe his nerves. When he finished eating he was taken back through the panel and placed once again into the non-sensation, suspended state. He did not try to resist. He wasn't afraid. The concern he had when he first realized he was in the presence of aliens had disappeared. A strange calm settled over him. He found he didn't worry about his crew searching for him. For the next several days he was studied, tested, observed, fed, suspended by his new friends. His emotions diminished as they were not heeded by any of the beings. He just went along with their searching, poking and prodding in the name of science.

Gerald was upset and confused. He could not locate 0-10. He had disappeared just like Martin. He toyed with the idea of sending another of the captain robots to Mars to replace 0-10 but talked himself out of doing so. He needed the other robots for a test landing and exploration of Indigo-35. There had to be other life forms on Mars and other planets. That stream around Martin took on a form and acted as though it had a mission. Perhaps Martin and 0-10 were being held captive. If they were being seen as invaders the entire fleet would have been attacked or destroyed. He had always hoped that more advanced life would not have the barbaric tendencies that many humans have on Earth. He wanted a Eutopia. If Mars and other planets could be populated, perhaps that new race of humans could be bred, or even programmed, to live together in harmony and peace. Systems were close to being ready to attempt the journey to Indigo-35. The wormhole had not been visible recently. There were increases in radioactive activity as well as a few sightings that could have been wormholes. The spaceships had been stocked, the rovers moved into the hatches, instruments checked and re-checked and the astronautical gear tested and readied for suiting up. Before the spacecraft and crew left the space station the capsules with their special selectivity coatings were positioned around the ships and the artificial universe pumped into the space between the ships and the capsules.

Day 329, November 1, 2015. Gerald was up at 5:00 am. He could not sleep. More convinced than ever that Martin and 0-10 had been taken to alien ships or cities on their planets, he wondered if there would be a way to communicate with these beings. Martin and 0-10 were being shown the advanced technology and introduced to the advanced intelligence of the Martians and Apellonauts. 0-10 was being programmed to be able to translate telepathic communication to the humans on the space station.

Martin was comfortable with remaining with the Apellonauts until they could teach him how humans could communicate with them. He realized they were curious and non-aggressive. They could be very helpful in aiding the Indigo entourage through the wormholes and to learn what would be needed to land, explore and live on Indigo-35, or Apello, as it was actually named.

Gerald showered and dressed, ate his dehydrated breakfast and floated toward the laboratory. His plan was to take a more critical look at the stream elements that were contained in the cannister attached to his spaceship. The other astronauts and scientists were still sleeping. The door to the laboratory was very thick. It took a fair amount of effort to open the door. Gerald had noticed some muscle wasting during this year in space despite eating well and exercising several times a day. He almost was knocked back into the anteroom between the sleeping quarters and the lab by none other than 0-10. There stood the robot, looking the same as usual- just standing in the doorway. Gerald almost hugged him, which would have been ridiculous.

"How did you get here?" As soon as he said it Gerald realized that 0-10 could read his thoughts.

"0-10 will bring a message from the Martians and Apellonauts to the leader of the space station."

Gerald could hardly contain his excitement.

"0-10 will show leader how to communicate with the aliens."

Gerald noticed a thin wire exiting the mainframe located in the back of 0-10. It appeared to be a cable connector for a computer. Gerald floated over to the computer bay. 0-10 obediently floated behind Gerald. Gerald hooked the cable into one of the computer ports. A series of digital shapes and odd figures covered the screen. Gerald gazed at the screen and then to 0-10. A form with a large head, several eyes and a cylindrical body came on the monitor screen. It stared at Gerald who seemed to be in a trance. 0-10 spoke in a low, monotone voice, different from the usual one that came from his computer.

We are the inhabitants of the planet you call Mars. We do not have human qualities like your robot. We are communicating telepathically to your robot. It has been programmed to translate what we say to you from our language to yours. Your robot is an interesting specimen. The Apellonauts are studying your human on one of their spaceships that observes your planet called Earth. Your human specimens are very primitive. Apellonauts are teaching the human how to translate their language into yours. They also are teaching it things about their planet, Apello. Direct your questions to your robot and he will communicate them to us. We will communicate our information to your robot.

Gerald didn't know where to start. He was speechless. Finally, he found his voice and asked 0-10 if the inhabitants of either planet could help his ships get through a wormhole and to the planet Apello.

To traverse a wormhole a mass must become exotic or negative gravity because the neck of all wormholes are composed of exotic mass and a positive mass would be destroyed if approaching this area. Our ships follow a stream of negative ions and fly into the center of that stream when traveling through the wormhole. Earthlings do not have such a device from what we have observed.

Gerald was proud of the work his SIES scientists and technicians had done. "There are scientists here on this space station who have found a selective osmosis substance from which we designed capsules to encircle the spaceships. When the ship enters the neck of the wormhole the artificial universe between the ship and the capsule will neutralize the negative gravity surrounding the capsule without effecting the negative gravity keeping the neck of the wormhole open."

Interesting. The Apellonauts can send a stream and a spaceship for your ships to navigate the wormhole if that would be acceptable.

"That would be so helpful! I will confer with the crew. How do you know when a wormhole is becoming visible?" Gerald's hands were shaking. He knew the crew would be getting up and he wanted to explain it to them before making a commitment. They might not believe him until they actually saw the Martians (inhabitants) and heard the communication through 0-10.

Wormholes have a radioactive signal that our instruments can detect. There is a pattern to the signals when they are able to be visualized. Our ships have a tracking system that can detect these wormholes, their position, size and stability even before they are seen on our monitors.

Erin and several of the crew members floated into the laboratory. Gerald put up his hand to have them remain silent. He said to 0-10, "0-10 will relay to the Martians that I need to take a few minutes to explain your return, the Martians and how we are communicating." 0-10 translated the message to the Martians. They agreed to remain on the computer while Gerald tried to explain the recent events. Erin and the crew were speechless. They stared at the Martians' image on the monitor and their jaws dropped. They kept looking back and forth between the computer monitor and 0-10 who stood tethered to the computer wearing his usual droll, non-blinking expression.

Erin spoke first. "Gerry, 0-10…esteemed Martians, I am so excited to meet you and communicate with you. How long have you, and others been observing planet Earth?" 0-10 translated.

We do not have the same time genre as Earth. Our days are similar in what you call "hours", but our "year" is much different. Other planets are very different from your calendar and time. It has been hundreds of your years that inhabitants from planets have conducted observation missions to planets and stars other than their own.

"Have there been wars between other planets' inhabitants?" One of the crew asked. Gerald scowled at the military crewman. He did not want the Martians to think earthlings thought about aggression.

War is not an option. There is no benefit to that activity. Hundreds of years ago when our inhabitants were primitive living celled beings there were arguments and emotions that led to war. As technology progressed those emotions and instincts were eliminated from the programs of the forms we present now. Inhabitants from other planets are at different stages of development. We have not encountered any that were aggressive. We debate without having to deal with emotions that complicate results. Why do you ask such a question? We will include the Apellonauts in this communication.

Gerald held his hand up to the crew member.

"Earth is a young world. We who chose this mission reject aggression. Our main goal is to learn from life forms, such as yourselves, and to advance beyond primitive behavior. We would like to hear from the Apellonauts as well. Do they communicate through 0-10 as well?" The crewman floated back toward the sleeping quarters.

Yes, we communicate in the same manner.

"Earth's scientists and astronauts are planning to send humans to your planet we call Mars to establish a home on the surface. We do not want your inhabitants to feel like we are invading your planet. If we can live in harmony with you and with inhabitants of other planets perhaps we can learn much from each other and breed peaceful "earthlings" similar to yourselves." Gerald told them.

Perhaps earthlings can show Apellonauts how to survive on the surface of our planet. We presently live deep within the recesses of what you call mountains. We have extracted an element from Earth's atmosphere called Nitrogen and combined it with elements from Apello to create a 78% concentration of the N element. We are in the process of building cities on the surface of our planet. We can use study of your human bodies to mimic qualities in Apellonauts that can exist in the surface atmosphere.

Henry was definitely interested.

Gerald asked if the Apellonauts that were studying Martin would allow him to converse with them.

We will bring the human here to speak with you.

Martin floated into the viewing area of their computers. He looked younger and very peaceful. He was wearing a filmy material that glistened when the lighting hit it.

"Hi, guys. I am having an amazing time with these new friends. They are treating me very well. They give me food and are teaching me amazing things about their development and technology. I also am eating the best food. The coffee is like nothing we have on Earth."

"Martin, have they told you how they transported you to their ship? We were devastated. Jack went out to help you when you seemed to be absorbed by shiny particles within the stream you pulled into the cannister on the side of our spacecraft. He still is fearful that the portion of the stream we still have in the cannister will attack us too." Gerald asked.

"Tell Jack and the other crew members there is nothing to fear. Those particles can transport objects from one place to another. It is almost like the ones we created in the movie Star-Trek. Remember "beam me up, Scottie."? I don't know how they do it. Their technology is beyond anything we have on Earth. My brain is swelling with information they are trying to teach me." Martin smiled and looked at the Apellonaut that was hovering behind him.

If you wish to have another human transported to our ship that human can release the stream from your cannister, and we can transport him to our ship. The Apellonauts offered.

Gerald didn't think Jack would want to be the one transported to an alien ship. He had one of the crew tell Jack what had been happening in the Laboratory. Jack floated into the room and stared at 0-10, the monitor with Martin smiling there and the spooky looking thing behind him. "Wow! Marty! I'm so glad you are okay! I can't believe all this! Am I dreaming or something?"

"No, Jack. This is very real. These robots are not aggressive. They are brilliant and have treated me with respect. I am learning so much. They, and others from planets where life exists in many dimensions have been observing our crazy planet for hundreds of years, " Martin explained. Jack had to strap himself in one of the chairs in the room. He was shocked. His heart was beating so fast he had to take several deep breaths and meditate to relax. He still was too fearful to volunteer to be absorbed on to an alien ship, despite Martin's calming demeanor.

Erin volunteered. She reasoned that the aliens might want a female human specimen to observe. Plus, she could bring forensic expertise into the mix. Gerald and Wayne agreed to help her perform the EVA in order to release the stream from the cannister. She had only practiced an EVA on the mountain in a controlled module. One of the other astronauts would accompany her to help with opening of the cannister. Henry had also wanted to be transported but was convinced by Gerald and Wayne that he would be critical to the journey in their spacecraft as they approached the wormhole.

Erin was nervous about going outside the space station and exposing herself to a transport method she knew nothing about. Blake Cameron, one of the crew members who was a seasoned pilot and astronaut helped Erin don her spacesuit and helmet. He tried to assure her that he would be guiding her through the EVA and would stay until she had been transported to the alien ship. He, too, was concerned about releasing the stream from its capsule and having no knowledge of the process used by the Apellonauts to transport a human from one place to another. Even though the Apellonauts seemed highly intelligent and non-aggressive he still was worried that Erin and Martin were being used experimentally by beings they knew very little about.

The hatch in the compression chamber was released and Erin and Blake floated outside the spacecraft which was still parked into the space station. Erin was in awe of the view into outer space. She took in a huge breath as the endless darkness wrapped itself around colorful stars and particles of space junk swirling in the abyss. Blake guided her along the outer portion of the ship. He made sure her tether did not catch on any of the jutting parts of the ship. Erin grabbed each handrail with a death grip. The cannister containing what remained of the stream looked monstrous to her as they approached it. Blake moved ahead of Erin so that he could use tools to unlatch the cannister. Erin's heartbeat was like a symphony of drums as Blake cautiously unlocked the six hinges. He radioed Erin that he was ready to open the cannister and she should take her place in front of the opening. This required she let go of the handrail she was clutching. Blake was to move a distance away from the cannister but remain close enough that he could observe Erin should things go south. Blake had not observed Martin being "absorbed" by the stream. He held his free hand over his laser gun just in case he would need to use it. A throbbing could be felt as the lid was raised. Blake moved a short distance away. Gerry and Henry were communication through 0-10 to the Apellonauts as to the timing of the cannister release.

Erin was surrounded by glistening particles so bright and colorful she had to close her eyes. A tingling feeling all over her body did not frighten her. She gradually became relaxed and peaceful in a way she could not describe. Blake watched in amazement as Erin's body melted into the stream. He could not see her face because of the helmet. Her body did not fight whatever was happening to her. The stream was filled with sparkling particles. Blake swore he could see the form of some kind of a being. It appeared to have a large head and a cylindrical body. Dark spots around its head flashed beams of light into space surrounding the stream. Erin disappeared. Blake could not move. The form in the stream seemed to be looking at him. The form melted into the stream which turned several shades of green and blue before it zoomed into space and disappeared. Blake shook his head and came out of a trance-like state. He moved cautiously toward the cannister to close it and lock it. He felt a calmness he had never felt before. Once his task was completed he leisurely moved along the spacecraft and into the pressurized compartment. He took off his space suit and helmet and exited the ship. When he floated into the space station lab area where Gerry, 0-10, Wayne, Henry, the Colonel and some of the crew members awaited his return he was met with a standing ovation. They all noticed the peaceful look on his face. He looked years younger.

"Well, Blake, what was it like out there? Did you experience anything odd or frightening?" Wayne asked.

"It was unbelievable! After Ms. Coutcher left, um…was absorbed by some sparkling particles in the stream I swear there was a.. not a person but a "form" that looked at me before the stream changed colors and took off into space. All of a sudden I felt warm and peaceful….so peaceful. I can't describe it. I still feel calm in a way I have never felt before." Blake looked around at everyone.

"That is how Martin is telling us he feels. He doesn't seem fearful of these aliens. He elected to stay with them so he and Erin can learn all they can about them. They seem not at all aggressive. They have been watching Earth and other planets and stars for hundreds of years." Henry looked at the monitor. 0-10 began to stare at the hieroglyphics on the screen and started to speak.

We have received your crew member, Erin, in our ship. We will not hurt anyone. We will answer their questions and study them for several of your days. It is understood that you need them to help with your mission to our planet. We will return them to you in five Earth days. There is no need to access the cannister, we are able to transport beings through any surface. When they arrive, they will have knowledge that will assist you to access and be transported through the wormhole. Will you agree to allow your robot to join us while we travel back to our planet? It can give you information that would be helpful preparing you for the rigors of wormhole travel on life forms and on robotic forms.

Gerald consulted Wayne and the pilots. They agreed that it would be advantageous to have a preview of what effects they would experiencing as they traveled through the wormhole. The only thing they would not have advanced knowledge of would be the emotional toll to which the crew would be subjected.

We agree to have 0-10 accompany you back to Apello. How will we be able to communicate with you since he is our interpreter?

Your humans, Erin and Martin, will have learned how to interpret our communication system to you and to us. We must warn you that the flight through a wormhole is extremely difficult and dangerous. Wormholes are fickle and unpredictable. When our Apellonauts were primitive and had live components there were many who vanished when arriving in the neck of the wormhole.

"We understand the dangers. We are very grateful for your advice and assistance. We will have 0-10 transported after Erin and Martin are back in the space station." Gerald made sure everyone agreed to the exchange and were still committed to complete the mission. He had given all the crew, pilots and scientists the option of remaining on the space station. No one opted to back out of the final leg of Indigo-35.

Erin could not feel her body. She tried to move but there was no feeling. She panicked and called out. She remembered the weird feeling of warmth and peace she had experienced when the stream took possession of her. The thumping sound grew louder as she gazed into the "eyes" of the Apellonaut that floated over to her. *Oh, my goodness! They are huge! They look almost transparent. I wonder if those are eyes in that big head? It is moving some kind of instrument over my body. Why can't I feel or move anything?!*

That voice like the one in the SIES lab that had instructed her every day came from somewhere in her brain. *We have suspended your body for a few hours so we can study it. Don't be afraid. We can interpret what you are thinking remotely through your robot. It is still on your spaceship. It will be transported to this ship to accompany us back to Apello (you call it Indigo) after we send you and Martin back to your ship in several of your*

Earth days. You humans eat food and drink liquids. When we have completed our investigation, do you want some food and beverage?

Erin was amazed at the kindness of the voice. It had the same tone as the one in the lab, but it was softer and more reassuring. She relaxed and said, *"Thank you. Food would be welcome after. Where is Martin?"*

The other human scientist, Martin, is in a class in another part of the ship. He will join you during the food and drink taking. You will attend classes also. Your technology is very primitive. We can help you assimilate to the environment of Apello if your ships and crew can survive the wormhole. We will help you. Why do you want to live on another planet?"

Erin wasn't sure why either. It had been difficult to make the decision to join the Indigo mission. Gerald had given all the scientists and technicians the option of remaining on Earth but amnesic to anything to do with Indigo. They also were encouraged to be part of a monumental attempt to inhabit and learn about other planets. The crew that decided or had been chosen to stay did not agree that Earth was in jeopardy of being eradicated in one-hundred and fifty years. They knew that eventually, possibly thousands of years in the future, that the Earth's orbit would gradually be so close to the sun it could be radiated and extinguished.

"I am a scientist as many of the rest of the Indigo's mission crew. We have always been passionate about discovering other forms of life in the universe. Many humans do not believe any other forms exist. We also know that we have been poor protectors of Earth's resources. We want to do better. What we learn on this mission may help those left on Earth to make changes to save our planet."

Hundreds of your years ago our primitive life forms made mistakes with our planet. Research discovered that these things called "brains" were saddled with "emotions". Those "emotions" were interfering with the science of living in violent and unfriendly atmosphere on Apello. Other planets with life forms had the same problem and were forced to live under the surface of the planets or be extinguished. Artificial Intelligence was rapidly developed, creating beings with advanced digital minds devoid of messy "emotions".

Erin and Martin were not only treated to excellent cuisine but were also given instructions in space travel, computer science and environmental science. Their brains were inundated with knowledge that was hundreds of years in advance of Earth's. The Apellonauts shared the dilemma of nitrogen levels on their planet and how they had assimilated those levels using Earth's atmosphere and bombardment with radioactive waves. Finding out that Indigo's atmosphere had a concentration of Nitrogen similar to Earth's made possibilities of human and plant life survival more realistic. After one Earth week the 0-10 and Erin, Martin exchange was agreed upon. Because the humans had emotions they felt sad that they couldn't stay longer. The Apellonauts had taught them all their human brains could absorb. The timing of the appearance of a wormhole large enough to transport the three ships in their capsules remained critical. The Apellonauts had expertise in evaluating the conditions alerting them to a wormhole's appearance. Their spacecraft lined up some distance away from the space station. Gerald's astronaut pilots readied the SIES spacecraft to be able to follow the alien ship into the mouth of the wormhole. Anticipation was at a pinnacle. Some of the crew were not totally trusting that the aliens meant them no harm. Earthlings often had trust issues just because they were human. Some feared, despite the lack of evidence, that the aliens were leading them into the wormhole to be destroyed. Gerald and Wayne knew that was always a possibility even before the Apellonauts appeared.

CHAPTER VIII

TEN TORNADOES

The three spacecraft stood silent and poised as their protective outer cladding was slowly assembled around them. The artificial universe created between the ships and the capsules enclosed the spaceships. This was a complex, meticulously timed operation, with each phase of the encapsulation requiring perfect synchronization. The launch pads were positioned so that the spacecraft would be pointing toward the Apellonaut spacecraft. Finally, the countdown began. Madeline, locked in her office staring at her computer. A special super-secure connection had been sent to her. It was one of the gems that the Apellonauts had shared with Erin and Martin. Utilizing radiation streams invisible to Earthlings, information—converted into streams of atomic particles—could be targeted to a specific receptor on her computer. Once the information was transmitted it would only be visible to the human eye for one hour. Madeline was an important part of the Indigo project despite not being able to actually be a part of the crew. At 9:00 pm, Earth time, she witnessed the three spacecraft in the launch pads of the space station as the countdown to ignition and take-off began. Ten, nine, eight—she was afraid to blink—seven... Her teammates from I-35, astronauts she had known from her years working at NASA and other crewmen were perched on a precipice that could lead to disaster or the making of history. Six—five—four—three—two (her heart beat so loudly she was certain it could be heard all over SIES)—one! Blast off! She watched as the three ships moved gracefully off the launch pads, their positioning rockets firing to keep them on course. Suddenly, they were swallowed into the darkness of space. The space station remained on the screen for several minutes and then there was nothing. She knew that if they made it through the wormhole and to Indigo-35 she would not be alive to hear about it. Unless there was some magical discovery securing longevity beyond one-hundred twenty years, she would be in heaven, if there was such a place.

The crew of the three SIES spaceships were filled with those dangerous emotions the Apellonauts purported to be scientifically inhibiting. Though they needed to keep their focus on positioning the ships behind the Apellonauts' ships before entering the wormhole they couldn't fully contain the storm of emotions filling their bodies and minds. This was the point of no return. They would either be living on a planet light-years away from Earth or be destroyed in the process to complete the mission. Remarkably, no member of the mission crew or science team elected to remain behind on the station. The communication process the Apellonauts had taught to Erin, Martin and 0-10 would hopefully be able to transmit the notes from their journey to the space station and then, in time, to Earth. Madeline was responsible for encrypting the information as long as she was still alive and able. Future information would be captured in time capsules automatically transported by rockets and housed under the SIES complexes.

These were timed and programmed to launch toward the space station near Mars should Earth or the complex be destroyed.

The Apellonauts' ships approached a dark object with irregular borders. It seemed to undulate, expand, and contract. Gerald and Wayne monitored the cameras as the image appeared and disappeared; each time, the black opening growing larger. They couldn't speak. The three SIES ships—the *R.D. Quincy*, the *EMS*, and the *Romer*—followed the Apellonauts' vessels. The pilots of the SIES ships received instructions translated into English from 0-10.

When your ship is within one-hundred yards of the wormhole's mouth, it will be pulled into the neck. Do not ignite any positional rockets. The vibration and turbulence will be violent. Do not touch any of your instruments or rockets. Stay strapped tightly to your seats. We understand that you have a negative atmosphere inside the capsule covering your ships. As soon as you visualize another mouth, the turbulence will decrease, and you will have to de-ionize your atmosphere surrounding your ships or you will be forced back into the neck and destroyed. Engage your positioning rockets as soon as the exit mouth appears. You will have entered a time warp that will propel your ships at 512,000 miles per hour. Everyone on the ships must enter the time capsule enclosures, lock them and sleep. When you awaken, you will be close to Apello and some other planets. You will be five years older but look the same essentially. The time capsule enclosures will open automatically if they have been programmed by your humans according to our instructions. Erin and Martin smiled confidently when the crew looked at them.

The pilots and crew strapped themselves into the seats when the ships reached the critical distance from the mouth. Their vital signs monitors displayed elevated heart rates and rapid breathing. All members of the SIES crew had dressed in the special spacesuits and helmets to prepare for the change in the artificial universe needed to pass through the neck of the wormhole. The sound began like thunder during a spring storm. It grew louder and deafening despite wearing helmets and being inside a ship covered with a universe and capsule. The ship began to spin. Each crew member felt a pressure in every part of their bodies. They still could breathe. The cabin lights flickered on and off as the ships were tossed inside a tunnel's tumultuous storm similar to multiple tornadoes. The straps holding the crew members stretched, almost to the snapping point. Tears ran down their faces and some lost consciousness. 0-10 translated instructions to the pilots to prepare to engage the positional rockets and to de-ionize the artificial universe. The pressure began to decrease. The ships righted themselves. The thundering noise retreated. The crew took their posts after tending to their members who were slowly regaining consciousness.

"I can't believe we survived that! It was like being carried away by ten tornadoes! I've never been in a tornado, but I can only imagine."

Gerald smiled and contacted the pilots, Erin and Martin and Henry in the other ships to make sure they were okay. "Good job! I know how frightening that was for me. You are very courageous." Gerald shook hands with the crew members in his lead ship, the *EMS*, before returning to the bank of computers in his lab after confirmation that the other ships were safe. He gave the orders to place the ships on autopilot following the path of the Apellonauts' ships. The pilots, crew, Erin, Gerald, Wayne, Henry and Martin entered their individual time capsule enclosures, locked them, and immediately fell into a hibernation-like sleep. Tubes connected to automated nutrient and waste ports were inserted into veins and somatic cavities to maintain life processes for the five-year journey.

CHAPTER IX

APELLO

The capsules hissed open, releasing their drowsy inhabitants. In silence, each crew member returned to their post. No one spoke unless giving an order or transmitting a calculation. The ships' interiors looked the same as when they had entered their capsules five light years ago. They all looked healthy and calm. The outside of the ships had been beaten up. Repair crews used small, tethered rocket-cameras to scan the ships' exteriors for damage. There didn't seem to be any significant damage to mechanical parts or computers. Most of the damage seemed to be cosmetic. It was decided to have the repair crew perform an EVA of each of the ships before they entered the atmosphere of Indigo. Gerald sent a message to the Apellonaut pilots through 0-10's translation port letting them know they would be performing the EVA. The aliens were confused. Their ships automatically repaired any damage via auto-sensors and a sophisticated robotic repair system. Gerald was sure they were amazed how primitive he and his fellow humans seemed. 0-10's human parts had gone through the wormhole without any serious complications. His heart rate and breathing showed no elevation during the journey. More proof to the aliens that these things called "emotions" were not practical. The SIES spaceships' pilots signaled they were ready to allow the Apellonauts to envelope their ships in a stream so that they could carry them safely to the atmosphere surrounding their planet.

Several days into the journey the SIES ship, Romer was hit with a large asteroid. The pilot, Colonel Steve Ague, used positioning rockets to avoid the asteroid, a maneuver that placed the ship outside the stream that kept it on course towards Indigo-35 (Apello). The Apellonauts saw that the Earthling's ship had left the stream. Gerald in EMS ship and Henry in R.D. Quincy had received the notification that Romer was in trouble. The Apellonauts sent one of their ships to help repair any damage to Romer. The stream was suspended, and the remaining ships held their positions while a large tear in the skin of the Romer was repaired in less than an hour. Wayne and Martin, aboard the Romer were amazed at the dexterity of the robot and some sort of beam emitting from its appendages that magically replaced the torn metal without the use of rivets or welding tools. The area that was repaired was not noticeable when the robot returned to the Apello ship by the same particulate method Martin, Erin and 0-10 had been transported. Jack remained hesitant to trust the Apellonauts. The traumatic experience watching Martin disassociate left him with Post-Traumatic Stress Disorder. He begged Steve, the pilot, to pull farther away from the stream. Steve would not disobey orders from Gerald or Wayne. Jack returned to his bedroom and grabbed a large metal wrench. When he was sure Steve was alone in the control compartment, he crept up behind Steve and struck him hard with the wrench. Steve slumped forward in the control chair. Jack's eyes were wild as he unbuckled Steve's harness and pushed him out of his chair on to the floor. Jack buckled himself into the chair and grabbed the controls. He activated the positioning rockets and headed the Romer towards the Apellonauts fleet of spaceships. He aimed the ship's laser cannons and fired toward the Apellonauts' fleet. Wayne and the rest of the crew were slammed against the walls of the laboratory compartment as the ship banked sharply to the right. The computer screens displayed the rockets heading toward the Apellonauts' ships. Wayne struggled to grab hold of the bars to pull himself into the control cabin. He couldn't imagine Steve doing something like this. Wayne hollered to two of the crew members to come with him. Martin tried to override the computer system on the rocket to divert it away from the Apello ships. When the rockets were launched a loud siren and flashing red lights inside the Romer marked a security alert. Wayne and the two crewmen reached the control compartment just as Jack reached for the pad to launch three more rockets. Wayne grabbed Jack's arm and another crew member tried to revive Steve. The second crew member unbuckled Jack and helped Wayne pull him out of the pilot's chair. The Romer was headed on a crash course toward one of the Apellonaut ships. Suddenly, all the Apello ships were cloaked in an invisible shield. Wayne jumped into the pilot seat and fired the positioning rockets to divert the ship to the left, hopefully away from the Apello ship.

Jack screamed, "They are going to turn us into robots! They are aliens! You must stop them!" The crewman holding Jack managed to secure his hands with a piece of wire. Jack began to sob and scream incoherently. Steve had a large gash on the left side of his head. The crewman helped him into the co-pilot seat and applied a compression bandage to the wound.

"What…what happened?" Steve mumbled.

"It's okay, Steve. Jack wasn't in his right mind. I steered the Romer away. He fired several rockets... he snapped. I think they didn't hit any of the alien ships. Do you feel okay to take over? I need to let the other SIES ships and he Apellonauts know what happened here." Steve nodded that he was okay to fly the ship. Wayne went back to the lab area and had Martin communicate with the other SIES ships and the Apellonauts that things were back under control.

The Apellonauts lifted the cloaking of their ships. *We don't understand why one of your crew would attack us. Our citizens do not attack any other beings or planets. We do have the capacity to destroy aggressors but have not had any occasions where that was needed. You need to reprogram that crewman.* Martin looked at Wayne and snickered. *Do you wish to continue with the plan to visit our planet?*

"We are deeply sorry for our crewman's actions. He was traumatized after watching Martin's transport to your ship. We are giving him some sedation and will monitor his actions throughout the rest of the journey. Yes, we do wish to re-enter the guidance stream and continue with the mission if you will have us." Wayne explained.

Very well. Head the ship toward the last Apello spacecraft in the stream and we will activate the inclusion process for your Romer ship. Wayne, Martin and the rest of the crew breathed a sigh of relief. They sedated Jack and secured him in one of the transition capsules. They attached the feeding, monitoring and elimination devices and disabled the inside locking device so Jack would not be able to escape. He would not be harmed by the confinement. It was their only option until they could complete the entering of Apello's atmosphere and send one of the captain robots onto the Apello surface along with two rovers.

No human from Earth had been this far in space. The colors of stars and suns were streaked with plumes of gaseous material and small swirling storms. Radiant beams slashed through the deepest black emptiness, the brightness piercing the air like giant swords. The photographs sent back to Earth were astounding. The crew of the SIES ships were mesmerized by the panorama. After several light years of travel there appeared on the observation screens a pink/orange glow surrounding a deep indigo blue planet. The shade of blue was unlike any seen on Earth. The surface looked like a large marble with specks of sparkling matter swirling within it. There were two suns that highlighted one portion of the planet as it slowly traveled in an elliptical path around them.

We have entered the atmosphere of Apello, our planet. You may position your ships in a row facing the solar side of the planet. We will be docking our ships on the surface in a station known as Arpegio. We will bring a docking station to your ships. When you have been positioned into the station you will be able to move from your ships into the protective compartments. There are supplies that you earthlings seem to need. Food substances, medical supplies and other articles Martin and Erin earthlings listed you will be needing. If you attempt to send any earthling to the surface of Apello you will need to alert us so that we can assist you in landing in as forgiving an area as possible. We can assure you the nitrogen levels are compatible with your Earth atmosphere. There is no element you call oxygen on Apello. For you to join our cities, you will need to have oxygen with you. You can then extract the nitrogen from our air and infuse it with the oxygen into your uniforms and helmets in order to meet with us. We have some cities being built on our surface. Some are complete. Please make sure there are no aggressive activities by your crew toward our citizens. They will be eliminated should any of that type of activity be noted.

"We will follow your instructions and intend no harm. The docking station is large enough to accommodate all three ships and our crew. How are you able to move such a large object from your planet to the atmosphere?" Wayne asked.

We are able to move any size object because our atmosphere has very little gravitational force and we can control the density of any object through our own computer-generated calculations. When you visit the surface, you must allow us to control the areas surrounding your space suits so that you can explore without shooting off the planet into space.

◄ ◄ ✖ ► ►

Emily, who had met Madeline during that exciting visit to Switzerland, had requested an appointment. Emily suspected that Gerald had plans beyond Mars even though he did not tell her about the full mission of Indigo-35. Madeline wanted to shout out to the world that SIES had traversed a wormhole, developed a relationship with aliens from a planet at the edge of the universe, managed to abort an attack on the aliens by a deranged SIES crewman and were forty-five light years away in space about to explore the Apellonauts' planet. No one would believe her. She would be seen as stark, raving mad. Of course, she would honor the secrecy of the mission. Madeline sighed and took a big gulp of her cold morning coffee as she told her secretary to bring Emily into her office.

Madeline offered her hand as she looked into Emily's beseeching gaze. "Hello, Mrs. Procter. It's a pleasure to see you again. Please have a

137

seat." Madeline gestured toward one of the two plush chairs facing her desk. "Can I offer you some coffee, tea or water?"

Emily sat in one of the chairs. "Thank you for the offer. I have already had much more coffee than I should ingest." She smiled and waited while Madeline moved from behind her desk and sat in the other chair next to Emily. "I appreciate you seeing me. I am sure you are very busy. Can I ask you the project on which you are working?"

Madeline looked surprised that Emily got to the point of her visit so quickly. "You don't waste any time, do you…may I call you Emily?"

"Yes, of course. I don't want to waste any of your time with small talk. When I visited you in Switzerland Gerald told me Indigo-35 had several goals. One, to test a surface agent that could filter chemicals through a process of computerized osmosis and two, to travel to Mars to place a space station satellite near the planet and to explore Mars. He told me it was to gain information about the planet in preparation for a planned mission to inhabit the planet with earthlings in 2025. I know my husband—my ex-husband. His passion for the unknown is unlike anyone else's I know. I very much doubt that was the entire reason for his behavior and the secrecy surrounding Indigo-35." Emily watched Madeline's facial expression which changed very little.

"Emily, Doctor Proctor is a genius. He has a deep passion for discovering ways to save our planet from the disasters resulting from climate change and global warming. I can only tell you that the main purpose of Indigo-35 is to gain knowledge of ways to make progress in those critical areas." Madeline had turned off her computer so that Emily could not see any of the images being sent to her by the Indigo crew.

"Madeline, why didn't you accompany them on their mission? If what you say is true, I know that you have a degree in environmental science and have been an avid advocate for climate change initiatives."

Madeline hesitated. "Yes, climate change research is one of my pet projects. I felt I could facilitate changes with the research from the Indigo project if I were here on Earth rather than out in….in a space station and on Mars. Emily, Gerald asked you to trust him. If he wanted you to know further details he would have told you. I trust that you would want to honor that request."

Emily felt her heart sink, "I am worried about him. I just need to know that he is alive. I am sorry to have taken up your time, Ms. Wilson." Emily stood and gathered her notebook and purse. She started toward the office door.

"Wait, Emily…. I need to show you something. You must swear that you will share this with no one, especially the press." Madeline moved to her computer. Emily walked over to stand next to her. The image of Apello appeared on the monitor. The blue colors of the solar and dark side of the planet moved gracefully amidst the soft pink haze surrounding it. Emily gazed at the beauty of the image. There were no colors she had ever seen to describe these.

"Oh, dear God! Where is this? Is Gerry taking these images? I have never seen anything more beautiful!" The image disappeared. Madeline took Emily's hand.

"Emily, Gerald loves you and your children more than anything… any mission. If you believe that, you will know that what he is doing is for you and all mankind. You cannot tell anyone what you have just seen. I know you are a journalist and want to write about this. All I can tell you it is research into particles in space that may contain information to save Earth and future generations." Madeline squeezed Emily's hand. Emily nodded and gave Madeline a hug.

Emily whispered, "I understand. I will only write what you have told me. If you communicate with Gerry tell him I love him and am so very proud of him." She smiled with tears in her eyes as she left Madeline's office. Her column in the Times the next day read-

Our planet, Earth, is suffering from the repercussions of progress without boundaries. Many scientists and lay persons have dedicated their lives to create ways to save this planet we love from destruction. Each one of us can contribute a small part toward this mission. Information gained from space research and missions to visit Mars, the moon and other sources in our universe can increase knowledge of survival tactics for our soil, our air and our bodies. The Times is dedicated to bringing every reader the sources available to make a difference. Listed below are several organizations that can assist each and every one of us with actions to decrease global warming and arrest climate change. Join me in this crusade.

◂ ◂ ✖ ▸ ▸

The docking station sent by the Apellonauts was much easier for the SIES spaceships to maneuver than the one near Mars. Once the ships were secure the crew entered the compartments of the station through a port that evaluated each of the crew's vital signs, their surface quality and their required atmosphere. When this was determined a green light flashed in the holding bay where the crew was being evaluated and they were moved through a wall that had no door. The main workroom was spacious, lined with banks of computers and plush chairs that adjusted automatically to the appropriate height for visualization individually. Soft lighting that seemed to come through the walls of the workroom was pleasing to the crew's eyes. There was no lack of gravity in the room so people could walk about without the weightlessness they experienced on their ships in space. After accessing different types of programs on the computers, the crew moved to the laboratory that was complete with equipment and chemicals needed for testing. There was a garden area surrounded by a capsule that allowed various types of gases to be mixed and tested to determine how plants would survive in various atmospheres. The next area was the living quarters. Each crew member had a private room for sleeping and performing individual tasks. There was an eating area with plush recliners with a computerized menu from which to order the food and drinks Earthlings needed. Each of the bedrooms had access to a shower and toilet that automatically cleaned itself with the touch of a button. The crew was amazed that the Apellonauts knew how to create such elaborate and appropriate accommodations for humans. Erin, Henry and Martin were pleased to be meeting together after the long voyage from Mars to Apello. Erin and Martin were anxious to meet with Gerald and Wayne to fill them in on their experience on the Apello ship. After a delicious lunch they all met in one of the "communication" areas in the living quarters. Each communication pod was equipped with computers, lounge chairs, refreshments and translation modules. Jack seemed to be resting comfortably in the spaceship's time capsule. His vital signs were stable, and his EEG (electroencephalogram) showed no spikes of aggression or distress.

"I am considering sending two rovers manned by the other two captains to Apello." Gerald offered after a couple of hours of valuable discussion. "We need to see samples of the planets soil, liquid matter, if any, air quality make-up and gravitational pull. One important sign we cannot expect to record is emotional state. Our robots may have human organs, but the brain is artificial intelligence and does not produce emotions."

"Gerald, would it be possible for one of us to accompany 0-11 or 0-12?" We have the suits and helmets that should protect us from excessive temperature variances, the Apellonauts can arrange for the information needed to assimilate to the weak gravity and our emotional and mental state could be monitored." Erin suggested.

Wayne interjected, "I am not comfortable with any of the crew visiting the planet until we have observed the captain robots exploration. This planet had barely any gravitational pull and we are not certain the Nitrogen in the air is the only chemical we will be extracting to combine with oxygen to keep our lungs alive."

"I agree with Wayne. I understand your enthusiasm to experiment with an actual human initially, but it presents with too many risks." Gerald smiled at Erin and Martin who seemed to have lost all fear of the unknown since their experience on the Apello ship.

"I will be testing various combinations of air as the captain robots breathe in the Apello atmosphere. We have already researched the chemical pattern of PP, the new gaseous chemical prevalent on Mars and Apello. By analysis of multiple combinations of gases with Nitrogen, Oxygen, PP and any other chemicals present in their atmosphere, I hope to be able to deliver air to human explorers that will support life with few side effects. The only thing I will not be able to test is the long-term effect of newly inhaled chemicals before a human exploration of the planet." Henry added.

Martin was the mediator between the polarized scientists. "Erin and I were impressed with the understanding the Apellonauts have for human life. They have this ability to list facts, calculate risk factors, perform a risk/benefit analysis within seconds. They agreed with using robot-humanoid subjects to perform the initial exploration, especially now that is has been proven the captain robots do not react emotionally. These aliens have data from hundreds of years of observations and morphological changes that prove emotions play a significant part in the survival ability of a being. Not that emotions are not important in the present state of live beings. We Earthlings may never wish to morph into AI robots." All agreed to spend several Earth weeks observing the SIES robots before attempting a human exploration of the planet. Gerald contacted the Apellonauts to apprise them of the SIES aliens' plan.

"We would like to thank you for the excellent docking station and accommodations. The food substances and amenities are superb. Our plan is to send two of our captain robots, similar to 0-10 robot, to the surface of Apello. They will be using rovers to gather samples from your air and surface environments. They also have humanoid characteristics and organs, but no source for emotions. Will you send coordinates for an appropriate landing site and what method to be used to allow the robots and rovers to remain on the planet? We see that you have several chemicals besides Nitrogen and PP in your atmosphere. Please send us any

information you have on the action, chemical pattern and characteristics of those chemicals or gases. We would need that information to prepare breathable air for the humans we send after this initial mission."

Your plan is acceptable. The list of elements and gaseous materials present in our air and soil are being sent to you. The landing site is also included. Your humanoid robots and rover equipment will meet with a team of examination Apellonauts. They will supply both of your explorers with a gravity module attached to them. This will need to be worn by any visitor and equipment. Apellonauts have a sustained gravity application as part of their make-up. Make sure there is no aggressive programming in either of your visiting robots. 0-10 had not demonstrated any aggression. It is interesting that the human organs are slowly atrophying as it spends time on our planet.

"Thank you for your assistance. We will alert you of the time we plan to send the robots and rovers. Can we use earth time for that notification?"

Yes. Perhaps the lack of endorphins in the humanoid portions of 0-10 allows his human organs to deteriorate.

"That is exactly what I felt might be the cause. What experience do you have with hormones?" Gerald asked.

We eliminated them along with other human characteristics and parts in the development of the present Apellonauts. The endorphins were kept in earlier models until we created a program that could replicate Apellonauts as needed. Your process of reproduction is flawed by genetic components and a thing called "relationships".

"Well, I certainly have to agree with that last statement." Gerald laughingly shared with the other scientists.

CHAPTER X

THE CITY OF APELLO

March 15, 2020. Gerald, Henry, Wayne, Martin, and Erin had worked feverishly on preparations for the initial exploratory mission. 0-11 and 0-12 had been examined, programmed and re-examined for any possible glitches that could abort the mission. The rovers were inspected, tested rigidly in storm tunnels created to mimic the storms on Apello and outfitted with storage cannisters for samples from the planet. The rocket that would launch both robots and rovers were placed on launching platforms. They contained enough fuel for both the landing and the return trips to the planet and back to the docking station. Erin was still hoping Gerald and Wayne would allow her or Martin to accompany the robots. Two elements that were not in Earth's table were extracted and analyzed. The first was named Xanthamo (X3). It appeared to have properties and a chemical imprint like Calcium. It was able to merge with N, O, and PP to form N2O2PPX3 that was tolerated by the lungs and heart. It could regulate heart rate and expand alveoli, reducing the necessary respiratory rate to as low as three breaths per minute. The vital capacity and the depth of the breaths was exponentially increased. Gaseous exchange was significantly improved and more efficient. There was an improvement in the osmotic selectivity of the blood/brain barrier, leading to improved cognition and lower REM sleep requirements. The only side effect was blurred vision. The second element was Porelite P3. This semi-inert element combined with Nitrogen and Xanthoma. P3NX3 was used by the Apellonauts to procreate. Depending on the number of "infant" aliens needed, the compound could be used three times per Apello year by each adult.

The Apellonauts would meet the module containing the two SIES robots, the rovers and equipment for analyzing samples. The designated landing area was at the base of a mountain not far from the entrances to the underground cities. The mountain would offer some protection from the frequent storms on Indigo-35 (Apello). An inflatable lab module would be set up near the mountain to be used to examine, catalogue and store samples. These would be taken back with the exploration craft and then to the Apello space station. Two earth weeks were planned for this first mission. If things went well Erin and/or Martin would be sent to the planet to spend one month living on the surface, visiting the Apello cities underground, on the surface and establishing a colony of structures to house future earth visitors from the SIES crew. It was very early in the morning when 0-11 and 0-12 were belted into their chairs in the space capsule. Two rovers were placed in the cargo area of the capsule, and it was attached to the booster rocket. After being fixed to the launchpad on the space station last-minute checks of all the systems were performed by the technicians in the crew. Gerald and Wayne monitored all the preparations to make sure everything would be done exactly as it would when real humans were sent to Apello. Erin and

146

Martin performed last minute checks inside the landing module, attached monitoring leads to the robots. Erin asked Martin to go to the lab for a computer card she needed. The lead technician announced the beginning of the countdown. A yellow light on the control center in the pilot's compartment flashed "Five minutes to blast off."

Erin knew the decision she was about to make would be seen by SIES command as grounds for dismissal, but she wanted to prove that robots, aliens and humans could live together in harmony. She moved 0-11 from his seat, took his spacesuit and helmet and put them on. She attached the monitoring lines to herself. She suspended 0-11's computer system to prevent him from reporting her. He was locked into one of the sleeping capsules. Erin had practiced meditating so that her vital signs would not change during the flight, despite her emotions. The red light flashed indicating the final countdown. Martin approached the launch area just in time for the hatches to close and lock and the barrier closed, barring admission to the area. Martin looked all around for Erin. He assumed she had gone back into the space station. After the module was launched Martin returned to his post. He oversaw sending orders to 0-11 and 12 for construction of the lab, living quarters and meeting with the Apellonauts.

Ten-nine-eight-seven-six. The red light began to flash. Sirens sounded marking the last five seconds until blastoff. Erin closed her eyes as the chairs tilted back into a supine position. She glanced at 0-12 who remained robotic. One last glance at the bank of instruments and computer screens in the cockpit. Erin allowed her breathing to deepen and slow as she envisioned walking in the warm sand along the ocean. Gentle waves kissed her bare feet and seagulls soared above in the icy blue sky. 0-12 stared unblinkingly at the ceiling of the cockpit. Five-four-three-two-one. Blast off! The liquid oxygen erupted inside the rocket launcher. Since the rocket was launched from a space station in the void, there was no sound. The crew, Martin, Wayne and Gerald watched as the rocket lifted off the space station and propelled the space capsule into the darkness. The chairs that held Erin and 0-12 returned to the sitting position. 0-12 took over the controls. One of the screens showed the timing of separation of the capsule from the rocket. The rocket positioned the capsule to head toward the solar surface of Apello. Cameras inside the cockpit scanned the controls and the two passengers. Martin froze one of the images because his heart pounded when what looked like Erin's face swept across his screen.

"Oh, my God!" Martin yelled to Gerald, "Erin…. Erin is in the space capsule! What the hell!" Gerald and Wayne ran over to gaze at the frozen image of the person behind the space helmet. It was difficult to confirm the image because of the blue tint of the face cover, but it definitely was not 0-11. "She asked me to get something from the lab while she stayed to check the harnesses and monitoring lines. When I returned with the stuff the capsule hatch was closing. I didn't see her around, so I assumed she had returned to her post. If that is her…. what in the heck was she thinking?"

Gerald grabbed a microphone from the desk and yelled, "Doctor Erin Coutcher…Doctor Erin Coutcher…report to the main laboratory immediately!"

"Sorry, Doctor Proctor, I'm a little busy helping 0-12 land this capsule. I know you all are really mad right now. I had to do this. We need to know how a real human will react to this planet. I am sorry." Erin's voice was steady and confident.

"You disobeyed my orders!" Gerald shouted into the transmission module as he stared angrily at the monitor. Erin's face shield opened as did

0-12's revealing their faces. "You had better know what you are doing." Gerald sighed. He knew Erin was the most competent human for the test landing and construction of the buildings should the test landing and subsequent experiences prove successful. "Very well, Erin. You have to follow my instructions should you survive the landing and other activities we rehearsed with the robots. Do you understand?" Martin and Wayne looked at each other and took their positions at their workstations. "Erin, I want you to take over the controls. You will have to re-program 0-12's computer so that he does not fight you for them. I am sending you the programming information on your interactive computer. By the way, where is 0-11? He is programmed to assist 0-12 with the landing and release of the rovers."

"Um—0-11 is deactivated in a sleep capsule. I de-programmed his system. Let me know the jobs he is to perform after I land this thing, sir." Erin reached over to 0-12, opened the door to his computer program apparatus and punched in the new information to allow her to land the capsule. The blue hue emitting from Apello was mesmerizing. There was no color like it on earth. Tiny flashes of diamond-like particles swept throughout the blue haze covering the surface of the planet. Erin positioned the capsule to head toward a semi-flat area near what appeared to be a mountain range just at the edge of the sun filled side of Apello. Erin heard the familiar voice of the Apellonaut direct her with coordinates toward the pre-determined destination. She did not need to have the SIES robots interpret for her since she and Martin had been trained to convert the Apello language into earth's English. As the capsule entered the atmosphere of Apello the particles and blue haze swirled around it. Erin had to use all the strength she could muster to hold the capsule in position to land at the pre-determined site. Sweat dripped from her forehead as she wrestled with the controls and flipped positioning buttons to slowly turn the capsule into a landing position. Dark blue pockets of swirling particles grabbed at the capsules hull pulling it very close to an ominous wall of the mountain at the edge of the landing site. No amount of meditation could control Erin's heart rate and breathing as she struggled to avoid crashing into the mountain. Through the darkness she saw what appeared to be a group of flashing lights.

Position your capsule to land between the spotlights. Our crew will surround the capsule with a gravitational stream. Before exiting the capsule, you will need to attach your lifeline to the port marked HA to the right of your chairs. We will infuse the chemical and gas combination your crew leaders have determined you will need in order to keep your lung structures viable. We see that there are three visitors on the mission. One of them is human as there have been spikes in the monitoring of what you call vital signs. Is there a human on this mission? The familiar Apellonaut voice queried.

"This is Erin. I joined the mission to accelerate exploration. My commanders are not happy with me. I hope you will accept me to set up a workstation and to learn more about you and your planet."

We do not understand the emotion "happy". It will be beneficial to learn how Erin tolerates Apello. In thirty of your earth minutes your space suits will contain enough of the mixture for breathing and you will be met at the exit port and fitted with a gravitational apparatus. Do not open the exit hatch until we give you the command to open. Will both robots be accompanying Erin?

"Yes, I will release 0-11 from his sleep capsule. He and 0-12 will need to have the breathing module attached. That can be accomplished in the thirty-minute period before arriving at the exit port."

That is agreeable with Apello landing crew.

Erin went back into the living quarters and opened the capsule containing 0-11. She initiated a program that would allow him to assist her and 0-12 in the exploration and set-up of modules for them to live and work on the planet. They would have to depend on the Apellonauts to add gravity and infusion ports to the lab and living quarters so they would be able to take off their spacesuits and helmets inside of them. Erin directed the robots to follow her to the exit port on the capsule. Once they had gravity, the Apellonauts would assist them in doing the same for the rovers. The living and working quarters were made of the same substance that surrounded their spaceships as they traveled through the wormhole. The substance, invented by I-18 team, could be expelled from large containers and the gravitational apparatus added to hold them in place on the surface. As Erin and the robots exited the capsule the brilliant blue dust swirled around their boots, sparkling like enchanted glitter. It was like walking in an enchanted land. The sky was filled with many colors. Blue, orange and green rays streamed in various patterns above them. The dust clouds lessened as they walked toward the mountain. The mountain seemed made of a spongy, deep-purple material, rising so high its peak vanished into the luminous sky. The Apellonauts met the three visitors on a flat surface where there were no dust particles. Lights suspended in the air surrounded the surface which ran for about a mile in every direction. Several of the Apellonauts assisted 0-12 to take the rovers down a ramp that eased its way down to the surface from a port in the side of the capsule. The Apellonauts surrounded the two rovers with the gravitational apparatus. Erin was amazed at how efficiently the aliens worked together. It seems like they intuitively knew what their job was through their telecommunication modems. 0-10 came from a passage that opened in the ground. He was accompanied by another team of Apellonauts. Erin greeted him but, of course, he didn't acknowledge her other than to look her way with his frozen stare. He and the new team from the city beneath the surface replaced the team that had assisted with the exiting of Erin, 0-11, 0-12 and the rovers. That team returned into the same passage that the new team and 0-10 had exited. It appeared that the ground opened and closed as soon as it was approached. There was no apparent opening until the group was ready to descend. The ground where the passageway appeared showed no visible signs of an entry port. Within a short period of time the buildings that would house Erin and her fellow robots were erected, secured with gravity and supplies from the capsule put in place in the buildings. The Apello workers retired to the underground city. Erin thanked them even though they did not need to be thanked. 0-10 went with the workers back to the city.

We will show you the above ground city as well and the cities underground tomorrow after you have performed your earthly exploratory duties. Do you have any questions? The Apello communication was interpreted by Erin.

"We have tons of questions, but we have several jobs we must do before we eat our dinner and retire. We will be ready by mid-day to see your cities. You have a wonderful work ethic. Thank you all for your assistance in setting up our little "town" on your planet." Erin telepathically sent back her message.

Apellonauts have been constructed to perform any work that is beneficial to other aliens and now, humans. We will send an exploration vehicle to take you to our cities at your mid-day during the light portion of our planet's "day". Evidently, a large moon passed between Apello's suns marking the "night" portion of their day. The "nights" were so black that a person could not see their hand in front of their face. There were stars everywhere. Thousands of tiny multicolored lights glistened high above the planet. The moon that hung between the suns gave off a muted blue halo of light around its perimeter but did not brighten the sky in any way. Erin watched as the sky gradually blackened and the eclipsed suns disappeared. How long the Apello nights would last was an unknown. The Apello communicator did not know why anyone would need to know that fact. When Erin asked that question, it replied,

We do not record such data. When the light reappears, we perform our duties. When it disappears, we become... inert. The communicator's tone was very matter of fact as if everyone should operate that way.

Erin and her robots sent messages to their crew in the space station. Gerald was ecstatic. The Apellonauts had helped to erect an exploration "town" for Erin. They began to extract samples from the air, the surface and the mountain to examine. Martin wanted even more than ever to be with Erin and the robots. He told Gerald he would like to pilot the next space capsule when it was planned. It had been decided that Erin and her robot team should spend at least two weeks with the Apellonauts. If all went well and her health was good, another capsule visit would be planned if the Apellonauts agreed. It was their planet and the SIES crew did not want to impose or threaten. It seemed earthlings were a curiosity for the Apellonauts. They were as interested in us as we were curious about them.

0-11 and 0-12 piloted the rovers and brought the samples to Erin in the newly constructed laboratory. The surface dust was rich in minerals, some of which were unknown to Erin. She sent photographs and microscopic images to the scientists in the space station. Even their research could not identify some of the substances in the samples. Erin took copious notes and lists of questions she wanted to ask the Apellonauts. The spongy material from the mountain had unusual qualities. It could withstand extreme temperatures without changing its composition. Though it appeared to be porous and soft it had the strength of Iron or steel. No amount of pressure could crush it or pulverize it. Erin and the robots grew tired. It had been a very eventful mission. Erin wanted to be rested for the visit the next day to the Apello cities. The darkness surrounded their dwellings and the three explorers slept. Erin awakened to the voice of the Apellonaut.

Dr. Coutcher, 0-11,0-12. There is a service of food and a substance called coffee in the exit hatch. When you are prepared to begin the trip to our cities, let your 0-10 communicate that to us. An observation vehicle will be standing by outside your exit hatch.

"Thank you for the breakfast food and especially for the coffee." Erin dressed after eating a delicious breakfast, programmed the robots to join her in the exit port and awaited the signal to open the hatch. She noticed the tracings of 0-11 and 0-12's vital signs were getting weaker. She adjusted the breathing apparatus on their spacesuits since they were only requiring two to three breaths to aerate their lungs. The gravitational apparatus was already attached to their suits. The port hatch opened, and Erin was amazed at the size and shape of the observation craft that awaited them. It was a glimmering silver oval ship with tinted blue windows all around. The craft was almost as large as the space capsule. It hovered noiselessly several feet

above the surface. A large opening appeared and a small Apellonaut motioned Erin and the robots into the interior. Soft iridescent lights shone from the walls, floor and ceiling of the craft. Transparent seats floated facing the windows and a soft whooshing sound flowed through the air.

Welcome to our observation craft. You may remove your spacesuits and helmets while you are in the craft. We have infused the air you need to perform the breathing function. 0-10 has assimilated, no longer needing his lungs and other organs. Soon your robots 0-11 and 0-12 will assimilate and their organs will atrophy. Erin, the human, will need less of the substances called "food" and "liquid". Human organs will continue to be needed presently. There is no way to predict if they will be needed over time as we have not had humans on our planet until now. Please sit on the floating seats and we will indicate the structures and surfaces on our planet. We are interested in observing your emotions, Dr. Couture, as you view various structures.

Erin, 0-11 and 0-12 removed their suits and helmets. The air they breathed was similar to that in the living and lab quarters they had constructed on the surface. It had a vague odor similar to mint and it was very easy to take extended, deep breaths. Erin's awareness was heightened, sounds and colors embellished, and she even felt a little lightheaded when she moved abruptly. The three visitors took their seats. There was no pressure on any part of their bodies though they were reclining. A pleasant sensation of warmth and gentle vibration relaxed Erin as she gazed into the panorama unfolding before her. The robots stared at the window, unfeelingly as ever. They had been programmed to document all that they observed so that the entire trip could be recorded and sent to the SIES team. The craft dove into the surface. Streams of blue and green with sparkling particles zoomed past the windows. The streams parted after several minutes of diving through them. Erin took in a huge breath as the city called Vota by the Apello voice appeared. It was enormous. Buildings shaped like snakes wound their way through the opening. Some were suspended high above others that tunneled into a powdery surface below them. Lights shone through the transparent walls of the buildings. Small oval objects about the size of a car whisked back and forth throughout the city. The observation craft moved toward a wall that absorbed the craft into another large opening filled with computer screens, Apellonauts working in front of them and box-like figures with large "feet" moved in and out of the work area.

You are in the city of Vota. There are ten undersurface cities on Apello. Each one accommodates a block of Apellonauts. A block is similar to earth's one-million humans. Because Apellonauts have not been able to adapt to the dark side of Apello we have populated all the undersurface space on the solar side of the planet. We have always been able to control the population until we began to explore the universe on the other side of the wormhole. It seems that something in the atmosphere surrounding your Earth and a few other planets with similar atmospheric consistencies has affected our reproduction apparatuses. Each time we telepathically order a duplication, it does not shut down when commanded until it has produced multiple Apellonauts. We never know how many will be produced. Each order produces a different number. Perhaps studying humans will allow us to remedy the situation. That is why we needed Earth's Nitrogen element concentration so that our Apello programs would not deteriorate, and we could build cities above the surface.

"I am struck by the efficiency with which your citizens work. Your telepathic communication is excellent. Humans have the ability to work

together in a similar fashion. One of the problems humans have is lack of clear communication which causes inefficiency, misunderstanding and aggression. If we can work together to learn methods of communication to better human interaction, we also might be able to discover why our atmosphere interfered with your reproductive programming. I'm sure you have researched the possibility that conversion to a different concentration of Nitrogen combined with the other elements in your atmosphere was causing the disturbance." Erin's scientific brain was racing through possibilities as soon as the Apello voice presented their problem.

Yes, we have researched and tested different chemical equations with the current and the former concentrations of Nitrogen. The only part of our construction that is affected by the Nitrogen change is the life of the programs not the area of our AI that controls reproduction. Your atmosphere has a layer called "ozone". It is a chemical that is deleterious in the human constructed form. Ozone is located naturally in the stratosphere. Its purpose is to absorb radiation emitted from your sun. Our explorers were ordered to remain in your planet's atmosphere only long enough to extract nitrogen. Our ships awaited the material extracted and placed it in cannisters on ships poised in the stratosphere. We have been testing combinations of Nitrogen 78% with O3 as well as other compounds. When the tour is completed we will take you to our testing laboratory in Vota. We ask that you work with our Apellonaut scientists for the rest of the day to see if you can help solve our problem.

"*I would be honored to work with your scientists. Yes, that would be agreeable.* Erin answered. *Could you answer some questions?*

What questions do you have?

"What type of material are your buildings, living quarters and other structures in your underground cities composed of? When did Artificial Intelligence replace other forms of Apellonauts? What powers your spacecraft for wormhole travel? What is the average lifespan of an Apellonaut? When an Apellonaut is no longer able to perform its duties or procreate, what happens to it? What is the composition of the gravitational support module? Are there any questions you have about our humans? Erin asked.

Our structures in the underground cities are the same as those we are constructing on the surface. The formula for the material is NPX3. It is a light, transparent, indelibly strong substance that is molded into pre-programmed shapes by a computerized directive. The apparatus that holds the compound is known as a "Postula Gun". Though it is only the size of a small rifle it is able to generate enough of the compound to create four structures. Reloading is done from ports located in the "walls" of the laboratories. The shape and thickness of the structure is programmed into the "guns" through a modem near the butt end of the apparatus. AI replaced more primitive forms of our inhabitants four hundred years ago. It was a gradual process. When we reach the surface city of Tora we will show you images of the progression over time. We do not use what you call "fuel" to power our spacecraft and other vehicles. They are all able to absorb molecules from the universe and combine them through laser technology to give off heat that propels our craft through space. In the wormhole, negative gravitational force in the neck is pulled into the spacecraft freezing the heated propellent. This suspends the ships in a time warp that allows it to journey as many light years as needed to reach a destination. Apellonauts exist for the lifetime needed to perform their duties.

Erin touched some dials in 0-11 and 0-12's computer systems to make sure the information she received from the Apellonauts was saved. Gerald and the other crew members would be thrilled to receive the answers to her questions. She tried to imagine what it would be like to be an Apellonaut, devoid of feelings and emotions, able to make difficult decisions and calculations and to perform daily until one was no longer needed. The aliens still possessed empathy, politeness and patience. They tolerated human iniquities and fumbles, provided food and shelter according to human needs and did not automatically react to Jack's attack. Perhaps they didn't realize these were human qualities they possess. These sometimes fall by the wayside too often on Earth. She watched as the ship roamed over the city. She hadn't seen anything that appeared to be water or plant life. Since Apellonauts did not need to eat or drink, she wondered how human food and fluid was obtained for them - a question for the next phase of the trip. The ship took a radical change in direction and speed. It climbed toward the surface so fast that the objects in the window were a blur. Suddenly brightness filled the panorama of the viewing area. Sparkling blue dust swirled around the ship once again. When the dust cleared a tall building surrounded by smaller units appeared.

We will be landing near the museum in the town of Tora in five minutes. The large building you see through the observation window is the Maxim. This houses the control center for programming Apellonauts and performing scientific experiments. These experiments advance our abilities to perform duties and enhance our capacity for learning. Please remain seated until 0-10 comes to guide you to the gravitation input port. Erin gazed at the building. It seemed to float above the surface. It had no windows. The entire structure was transparent though there seemed to be a covering that did not allow a visual of the actual floors or offices (if there were any). The building was shaped like a huge egg. There didn't appear to be an entrance or exit.

CHAPTER XI

HUMAN ERROR

The SIES crew were preparing to retire. It had been a full day. Technicians worked with Wayne and Martin examining the photographs and research Erin and the robots performed on Apello. Gerald joined in the crew's enthusiasm over the samples of material from the planet. When he received the information from Erin while she was on her exploration of the Apellonauts' cities, he felt they had been accepted by the aliens. He was so hyped up; he couldn't even think of sleeping. He paced from one workstation to another, peering at pages of formulas and observation notes. The intelligence of the Apellonauts as well as their acceptance of the invasion of humans into their very organized life surprised him most of all. He knew he needed to rest. As he walked through the room containing the suspension capsules, he went over to the capsule to check on Jack. He would have to decide whether he could allow him to resume his duties. There was no therapist with the crew to address PTSD or other psychological issues. He made a mental note: future crews needed a therapist, if human life on other planets became a reality. Perhaps the idea of eliminating emotions was not as far-fetched as it seemed. Jack's capsule was number thirty-one. Gerald passed the empty capsules lost in thought. He realized he must have gone past Jack's capsule when he arrived at the end of the row marked thirty to thirty-nine. He backtracked until he stood in front of the empty capsule that had contained the suspended crewman. He looked around the room and stared again at the empty capsule. His pulse pounded as he ran up and down the rows, the capsules looking like burial caskets to him all of a sudden. Gerald peered into two small rooms filled with equipment that monitored the environment and vital signs of the crew when housed in the capsules. His eyes scanned the panels looking for the screen shot of capsule thirty-one. The graph showed a regular heart rhythm, respiration and adequate environmental air. *How can that be? There is no one in Jack's capsule!*

Jack had used the metal phalange from his belt buckle to pry open and interrupt the locking system of his capsule. His eyes glowed brilliant red, and his muscles swelled, straining against his uniform. His only thought was to attack. The grotesque memory of Martin consumed by the stream fueled him as he slithered into a closet near the laboratory. He had to get into the one of the cockpits of the spaceships without being discovered. His hearing and vision was extremely acute. Every sound and image was louder and brighter than normal. He only had to breathe a few times per minute and his heartbeat very slowly with a much greater force than normal. It seemed as though some other force was controlling him. Gerald had informed the rest of the crew that somehow Jack had gotten out of his capsule. He didn't want to push an alarm to let Jack know he had found him missing. Jack watched as crew members searched the living quarters and the lab. He moved to the side of the closet when one of the crew opened the door but didn't see him. When the group had moved on Jack slipped out of the closet and passed cautiously by the living quarters. He passed a mirror at the hall's end—it showed only the empty corridor behind him. Invisible. To test if that was really true he ducked behind one of the bedroom doors. Max, one of the technicians was headed into that room. Jack jumped out from behind the door. Max did not seem to see him and continued to take out a small box from a drawer. Jack wrapped his huge hands around the poor technician's neck and squeezed. Max's eyes bulged and his body when limp. The box dropped to the floor. Jack felt nothing. The man who had been friends with Max for years was gone. He shoved Max's limp body under the bed. He picked up the box and looked inside. There was a pin in the shape of a butterfly. It was iridescent blue and green. Those colors burned into the already frightening image of Martin being devoured by the green and blue stream. Jack crushed the box and butterfly in his hand. The pieces dropped to the floor. Max's wife loved butterflies and he had bought that for her hoping that someday he might return to Earth to give it to her. Fortified with his invisibility, Jack passed through the crew, Gerald and Wayne rushing around the space station looking for him. The pounding of his heart grew louder in his ears as he headed for the launch area where the SIES spaceships rested. Suddenly, the red alert lights flashed, and the sound of the alarm blared throughout the station. Jack smashed his fist into the alarm pad in the Romer cockpit. He began to flip switches and dial controls that would start the fuel injection system to fill the rocket launchers. Gerald and the rest of the crew heard the roar of the injectors and ran toward the launch pad just as Jack strapped himself into the pilot seat and moved the control bar forward to launch the Romer into space. Gerald ordered Colonel Vandercook to take the *EMS* and destroy the *Romer*. It was the only way he knew to stop Jack who now was headed toward Apello. Wayne and the other pilots tried to contact Jack in the Romer, but he had disengaged the communication system. Colonel Vandercook ran into the cockpit, adorned his spacesuit and helmet, engaged the ignition system and launched the EMS into space.

Agitation surged through Jack. His thoughts raced erratically; his hands fired positioning rockets at random. He could not focus. He could see the planet Apello, but it seemed to be moving in and out of his field of vision, though it was his piloting that was the cause of the confusion. Without a clear aim and still several miles from the planet's atmosphere he fired missiles that missed Apello entirely, speeding into the void. Colonel Vandercook finally could see Romer heading haphazardly toward Apello.

Erin heard the low hum above the observation ship where she and the two robots were preparing to be fitted with the gravitational modem for their tour of Tora. Two Apellonauts came into the exit port and requested Erin and her sidekicks return to their seats in the main observation area. Erin asked why they were not continuing with the tour, but the two ushers did not answer. Above the window a huge spacecraft shaped very differently from the other Apello ships she had seen zipped into space. It was followed by several other smaller ships with the same torpedo-like shape as the large one. Each ship sped into the dark sky so rapidly she could barely make out what it was.

One of your spacecraft is on a trajectory toward our planet. It has released some aggressive rockets but has missed hitting the surface or any of our above surface cities. Do you have information about this aggressive activity, Doctor Coutcher? The Apello voice informed Erin.

Erin was shocked. She couldn't imagine why any of the SIES crew or leaders would be attacking the Apellonauts. *"I am not aware of any attack or aggressive acts. Please believe me. We would not risk the relationship we have enjoyed. There must be an explanation. If there is a computer available, I will contact my Leader to find out what is going on."* The entire observation ship vibrated as an enormous flash of light covered the window of the ship. Erin and the robots were thrown off their translucent chairs onto the floor. The two Apellonauts that had ushered them into their seats assisted them off the floor. Some distance away from the ship a cavernous hole emitted black smoke where the Maxim building had once stood. The Apellonauts' ocular sensors spun. Their arms swung erratically, and their tails thrashed against the floor. Laser guns moved from somewhere inside their arms into their long fingers of each hand. They aimed the guns at Erin, 0-11 and 0-12. Erin screamed and ran to a large square structure with a bank of computers embedded inside, the robots obediently following her. Laser beams spouted from the guns as the two Apellonauts swirled about the room. They appeared to be getting smaller as they swirled. Erin watched in horror. She managed to reach one of the computers and attempted to contact the SIES crew on the space station.

Jack no longer looked human. His face was contorted, and his eyes bulged. Flashing red particles oozed from his face and his body tore his spacesuit apart as it engorged with a green fluid. He could no longer reach any of the controls on the ship as it plummeted toward Apello. The EMS ship caught sight of the Romer heading toward Apello. Colonel Vandercook aimed as best he could at the spacecraft with two of his ship's rockets. Three Apello fighter ships headed toward the Romer. They enacted their cloaking shields just as the rockets hit Romer and Jack. Romer disintegrated and the

Apello fighter ships headed toward EMS. Ron Vandercook did not have the capability to communicate with the Apello ships even if he could see them.

Erin got through to Gerald. Martin was able to translate an urgent message to the Apello ships just as they were aiming their lasers at EMS. They uncloaked and veered past EMS as Ron watched them come very close to his ship.

"Wow! I didn't see those ships at all!" Ron reported to Gerald. "I feel awful having to shoot down a comrade and one of our own ships."

"Colonel. You did what you had to do. We have to find out why Jack changed and morphed into a terrorist. Return to the space station and we will debrief you after I have spoken with the Apellonauts." Gerald attempted to contact Erin who was now standing in front of several of the Apello leaders. The hole where the Maxim building stood had begun to rebuild. Several Apellonauts sprayed the substance that was used to build structures. Only a few of the younger Apellonauts' systems had been damaged when Jack's rockets hit the planet. Erin was told these were able to be repaired. She explained that she had no knowledge of who form SIES or why they would attack Apello. She asked permission to contact Gerald and Wayne to get information on the attack. She apologized profoundly even though there was none of that type of action in the Apellonauts' make up. The Apello leaders watched and listened to the interpretation of Gerald's explanation of Jack's unusual escape and morphological change.

We accept what you call an apology. Did this human ingest any of the transportation particles when he observed Martin being transported? If there was any breach in his helmet and particles entered his human body it would transform him into a primitive form.

"That is very interesting. Would that have happened to anyone ingesting particles from that mode of transportation? We will check Jack's suit and helmet for any breaches. Why are the particles dangerous in that way?" Martin translated from Gerald.

When the transportation streams were developed centuries ago the Apellonauts had to implant historical mutation phases in order to have an entire being or alien transported completely. The particles were developed to rapidly extricate all phases of development during the transport. Since Apellonauts and other inhabitants of planets do not have human parts the breathing and swallowing functions were not tested. Your human who attacked us may have taken on a primitive form similar to our primitive forms who were very aggressive. Now that you have experienced such a side effect we will change the composition of the particles to eliminate the side effect to humans. Our workers will have the Maxim constructed in one Apello day. We can begin to work on the problem when that is completed. We will need to use Dr. Coutcher to test our findings.

Erin watched as Gerald and Martin started to object. *"I will be available for any assistance with the particle project. It is the least we humans can do after attacking your city and destroying Maxim."* She made the "silence" hand gesture to the two men on the screen.

We will take Dr. Coutcher and robots back to their quarters. Tomorrow we will bring you to the Maxim for study. Your robots can remain in your quarters.

"Will I be able to communicate with you during the testing? If I will be sedated and cannot speak to you, I will need a robot to speak for me. Erin stated.

There may be a need to sedate you. Bring one of your robots.

"Thank you." Erin spoke with Gerald and Martin before she signed off. "I will program 0-11 to be able to mimic any thoughts I might have during the testing phase when I may not be awake."

"Erin, you do not have to do this." Both Gerald and Martin pleaded with her. "We can bring you back here and they can use 0-10 or one of the other robots to take part in the test since they have human organs."

"The robots' organs have no human evolutional history. It would not be a valid situation. I need to do this. We have attacked the very beings with which we will co-habitate. I trust them, Gerald and Martin. You need to do the same." Erin was directed to her observation seat. The computer screen shut down.

Madeline was engrossed in the communications she was receiving from SIES crew in deep space. She had aged and was now 75 years old. Someone would have to take over her position should she become unable to perform as she aged or expired. All of the information was saved on computer zip drive and stored in a vault hidden in a stone cellar beneath the SIES building. The Earth had become increasingly hot. There were hardly any Winter or Fall seasons. Many countries had been completely or partially buried by hurricanes and tidal waves. The east and west coast of the United States had gradually been diminished requiring masses of people in coastal towns to move inland. SIES and the businesses and citizens that had survived the hurricanes and flooding had all moved inland. SIES headquarters was now located in Memphis Tennessee. Most older people had to spend most of their time indoors because of the extreme heat. SIES and other structures were built on stilts to attempt to survive the ever-rising lakes and seas as well as the violent storms. The polar ice caps were almost completely melted. Wildlife such as penguins, polar bears, otters and sea lions were now extinct or endangered. If inhabitants needed to be outdoors, they had to wear protective masks issued by the new government environmental departments in each community. Many businesses no longer existed. Restaurants, bars, salons, museums, parks all were things of the past. Madeline's report depicted a grim, deteriorating Earth. Two missions to take inhabitants to Mars had failed miserably. There was one more mission that was scheduled for the next month. The failures were attributed to overheating of the outer covering of the space module. SIES and a couple of other scientific and environmental firms still operating were working with NASA to develop an alloy that could withstand the extreme heat the space module experienced when entering Mars atmosphere. The Martians had been receptive to having earthlings live on their planet. They were very interested in human beings since the experience with the SIES astronauts. Madeline had left detailed instructions about Gerald's mission and where to locate the zip drives containing all the information sent to her. There was some hope that she would be chosen to be a part of the crew sent on its third attempt to Mars. Perhaps if that mission were successful an attempt to travel to Apello could be created. Emily and Madeline had kept in touch over the years. Emily had been judicious in keeping her promise that she would only report suggestions learned from SIES explorers to help save the Earth from being destroyed by human stubbornness. She had just retired wanting to spend more time with her children, grandchildren and great-grandchildren. Gerald had sent his love to Emily over the years through Madeline. His heart was sickened to learn that mankind had paid little attention to the suggestions he communicated. He was learning details about filtration, chemical and atmospheric solutions to climate change, special ways to produce and store food products and space travel. He wanted to share all he had learned with his fellow humans on Earth. Knowing that they would have a difficult time believing that there had been a mission through time on the other side of a wormhole he relied on Madeline and Erin to filter the information in a believable manner.

The Apellonauts and the Martians had found a way to produce the food substances that humans needed to live. They harvested the spongy substance from the mountains on both planets, exposed it to a laser bombardment and a liquid similar to water, compacted the compound with various elements found in plant life and returned it to a "soil" from the surface of their planets in a huge laboratory that filtered ultraviolet rays from each planet's sun. Meat was produced by a mixture of tofu, nuts and the strange water-like liquid. It tasted just like beef without the properties that were injurious to humans. The Apellonauts and Martians would be teaching humans how to produce food in the same manner once they successfully joined them to live on their planets. There were other planets in the universe that had various types of inhabitants. Some were very aggressive, but most did not possess that characteristic. Travel to these other planets was rare. The benefit of visiting other alien societies was not balanced by the danger in space travel. The Apellonauts came to Earth to study humans and extract the nitrogen necessary for their surface colonization. The title, Indigo-35 had been re-assigned to identify the entire SIES mission since Apello was the actual name for the planet.

Erin had been escorted to the newly built Maxim building. The outside of the building still appeared transparent with no doors or windows or actual visualization of the insides. She was impressed by the quiet and efficient use of space. The entrance appeared when anyone approached the front of the structure displaying a password with digital signs. The entrance was sparkling with diamond shaped ceilings and walls that moved aside when approached opening into various "rooms". The walls of the rooms were made of the same material as the outside of the building. Each of the rooms contained equipment, banks of computers and a gentle whooshing sound that was very relaxing. There were no chairs. The Apello workers moved about by some type of mechanism in their tails. Erin was taken to a large room with walls that emitted a blue light and several recliners that could be moved into different positions. Large metallic funnels suspended in the air hung over the recliners and computer screens harbored images of the universe in slow motion.

Dr. Coutcher. You will enter the door marked with a crescent shape. A worker will assist you in changing into a garment that will allow us visualization of your organs as we test their reaction to particles. You will not be endangered. Monitoring and osmotic nourishment will be provided. Your robot will follow the workers who will be performing the tests to translate any thoughts you might be having that require a response. The sedation will render you in a similar suspended state to the one Apellonauts use for their rest periods. No human has been placed in this suspended state. We will be able to monitor your brain activity. If there seems to be any adverse effects from the sedation, we will abort the test.

"*I am confident that you will keep me safe. I hope you can reformulate the particles to prevent another transformation like Jack's. He was a very passive man that had no control over his actions following his experience outside the spaceship when Martin was transported. My fellow astronauts did find a small breach in the seam of Jack's helmet. That might have been the route that the particles entered and were breathed into his body. Will you allow 0-11 to translate your progress and findings to my superiors on the space station? I know you do not have the emotion called "worry" in your make-up, but my fellow crewmen and superiors are worried about my being used in this testing process."*

We will allow the robot, 0-11, to transmit during the testing. Go now to the changing area. A translator will assist you as you change. When you have completed the changing process, you will be escorted to one of the recliners in the center of the laboratory. Erin did as she was directed. She changed into a very comfortable feeling garment. The Apello worker who assisted her in the changing area had covered its several "eyes" with an opaque film. It did not seem to change its ability to function. Perhaps it was just an exercise to make her feel she wasn't being observed while undressing. After changing the Apellonaut escorted Erin to a recliner. Several taller Apellonauts approached her. One of them pulled a funnel over her. She was asked to close her eyes and breathe slowly. Her body began to relax. A feeling of being suspended flooded her body and she felt herself melt into a deep sleep. She did not sense any part of her body. She could hear the gentle whooshing sound swirl around her. The Apello scientists hovered over her. The garment she wore projected her internal organs, including her brain onto a large screen on the funnel. The lower portion of the funnel began to open and a small green stream with the sparkling particles began to fall into her exposed organs. The scientists performing the testing touched the screen and microscopic images of the cellular structure of each organ were projected sequentially as the particles infused into the cell. The cells in her brain and endocrine (secretory glandular) organs contracted as soon as a particle entered their cell body. Other organs' cells blocked the particles. The scientists examined the microscopic image of the particles in the affected organs and saw that they had appendages that the particles in the unaffected organs did not have. The scientists concluded that a protein substance in the particulate structure prompted the appendages needed to invade the brain and glandular organs of humans. After several attempts they preceded to eliminate the protein by exposing it to a fractional ray. These types of rays were unknown to Earthlings and also to other alien societies. They were manufactured by the Apello aliens who used them in repairing damages on their spacecraft. Several earthling hours passed before the correct exposure to the rays rendered the projectile characteristic of the particles obliterated. The funnel over Erin was repositioned to its suspended distance above her. She was allowed to "sleep" in the recliner the rest of the day. 0-11 stood nearby and translated answers to her questions about the findings that her brain was asking, even though it appeared she was asleep. Evidently, being suspended was quite different than sleeping or under anesthesia on Earth. 0-11 transmitted the findings to the SIES crew. Gerald, Wayne and especially Martin were relieved to see Erin resting quietly without any apparent side effects. They were excited to hear how the Apello scientists performed their testing without any trauma to Erin. Martin translated that Erin would be taken out of the suspended state the next morning. They would need to continue to observe and monitor her during that time to make sure she had no untoward side effects. The findings were sent to the area in Maxim that produces the particles used in the various streams so that the protein would be eliminated in the production process.

Martin became more anxious to be part of human life on Apello. He also had begun to have deeper feelings for Erin. Her beauty initially attracted him to her from the first encounter at SIES laboratory back on Earth. As they worked together, he was impressed by her intelligence, courage and sense of humor. They worked well together. Since being transported to the Apello spaceship and exposed to the same education and skills they received from the aliens he had fallen in love with her. Watching her resting tranquilly on the monitor he wanted to be lying next to her, sharing everything she was experiencing. The part of his character that obeyed all the rules, the tendency to take the safe route to everything in his life seemed to have changed. His hesitations and fears were gone. He felt a magnetic force pulling him toward Apello and toward Erin. Gerald and Wayne wanted Erin to be observed for another two weeks before a second space capsule with Martin as the pilot would be sent to the planet. Since discovering the robots' human organs were atrophying, they wanted to make sure humans would not be experiencing the same decay. Perhaps the type of air supplied to Erin's helmet and routed into her living and work quarters contained something that effected human cells causing them to shrink. The organs in the robots were kept alive and functioning by programs. Erin's and other humans' organs were controlled by electrolyte composition, neurogenic activity and cell metabolism, very different from the way robots' organs performed. Now that Erin had been exposed to rogue particles during the testing, they would have to monitor her to see if the exposure had affected her organ function. They already had seen that the respiratory and cardiac functions were changed by the atmosphere the aliens provided for Erin. Her respirations and heart rates were diminished by almost 75% but her circulation and oxygenation remained adequate. She required much less sleep and had increased strength and mental acuity. Since Martin could speak the Apello communication language he contacted the "voice" Apellonaut with whom he communicated most often. There seemed to be some type of hierarchy in the Apello population though there were no titles other than "worker" and "scientist".

"This is Martin, Dr. Szechnick. I am the SIES astronaut you brought to your spaceship and educated about your communication system and other processes. I have been observing the particle testing you are performing with Dr. Coutcher to discover a way to eliminate the side effects to humans if any are ingested. Since I understand the make-up of your substances, would you accept my joining you in performing these tests. I can take a space capsule to Apello from the space station in the next couple of days."

We will accept your assistance. We have found a protein that was causing the aberrancy. Dr. Coutcher will need to be observed for several of your days. It would be beneficial for you to observe her. Apello workers and scientists have repairs to perform for the damages remaining after the aggressive incident by your Earthling. Here are the coordinates of the landing site. Send your exact time of blast off. You will be met by two Apello workers who will bring you to Maxim, the testing site. The Apello voice replied.

Martin told Gerald, Wayne and Henry that he was going to repair a defective positioning module in one of the two remaining space capsules. It would take two days to perform the repair. He would not need any assistance. He carefully smuggled supplies and other items needed for a mission to Apello. Feeling guilty about disobeying orders he rationalized the need to be part of the Apello culture and their need of his expertise in testing. Ever since his initial experience with the aliens he had a strong urge to join them once again. He planned to take off during the night while most of the crew slept. It was three o'clock in the morning. Martin quietly left his living quarters after placing some duffel bags under his sheets. The hum of the ventilation system muffled his footsteps as he headed through the lab and other work areas to the space capsule on the launch pad. He would have to avoid placing any monitoring leads on his body so that his presence in the cockpit would not be noticed until after the launch. There was no way to eliminate or muffle the blast off. He would be part of the way to Apello's atmosphere before anyone in the space station would realize he had left.

On Earth Senator Wilson Eddleman and Richard Quincy had been contacted by Madeline. She had received the communication from the Martian Space Station that SIES ships had made it through a wormhole in space, parked in a space station within the atmosphere of Indigo-35, now known as Apello. This planet was similar in size and distance from its two suns as Earth. Its inhabitants were Artificial Intelligence prototypes that were very receptive to humans. Though they did not look at all like humans or have any human organs, they were extremely intelligent, non-aggressive and thousands of years ahead of us in technology. They lived under the surface of the planet in cities. They had sent spaceships to Earth's atmosphere to extract Nitrogen needed to allow them to build cities on the surface of their planet. Two of the human astronaut scientists from the SIES mission had visited with the Apellonauts and learned to translate their language into ours as well as many other interesting processes. The aliens assisted one of the female scientists, Dr. Erin Coutcher, to establish a colony on the surface of the planet, arranged for gravitational adaptation since their gravity is very minimal, and provided a breathable source for the human accommodations and for their exploration of the planet. This information was coming to Madeline during the past fifteen earth years. Gerald knew that she would need to retire soon. He wanted to make sure the two men who had facilitated the mission had the information they could pass on to people at NASA. He trusted that it would be used for the Mars mission only.

Richard and the Senator were growing old themselves. They asked Madeline to send information about the mission to Mars by the SIES astronauts and of the status of the Earth. There had been significant global warming. Both East and West coast states had been obliterated. The average temperature on a cool day was 110-130 degrees. Many species of wildlife were extinct. Ravaging tornadoes, hurricanes, earthquakes and wildfires had extinguished many areas of the remaining states and other countries were experiencing the same nightmares. Fresh water supplies were diminishing. Many people all over the world had died from dehydration or had been killed in fights over the water that remained. It was 2025 in Earth years. NASA was still preparing to launch several spaceships with the capacity to hold 150 people each to travel to Mars. Madeline's information would be critical to their survival. Gerald was adamant that the Martians and Apellonauts were not aggressive. Even when there had been a couple of accidental attacks on them, they did not retaliate. He told the NASA team that they absolutely had to approach these beings with respect and an open mind. The aliens had been observing us for hundreds of years. Their technological advancement was beyond our wildest dreams. One very interesting thing they had learned was that emotions often caused problems. Their creators had not put any emotions into their programs, but they all were polite, respectful, accommodating and extremely intelligent. They are very curious about us and our primitive ways. Gerald suggested two of the top scientists who also were decorated soldiers in the administration at NASA to be passed the information. The seven hundred people who had volunteered had diminished to 524 through deaths, hesitancy to take the risks involved and fear of their concept of aliens. Many of the conflicts over racism had disappeared or been resolved as the Earth's population diminished and basic needs to survive took precedence. Some good can come from bad situations. Societal divisions were a thing of the past as people had to rely on one another to survive. Though battles had erupted as the water and food supply became scarce, the discrimination based on race, religion, politics, ethnicity and gender had declined. Many people had begun to build underground cities and aquatic modules beneath the oceans in order to survive the heat. The press had been gagged from over reporting the doom and gloom. They reported on the good things that people were doing to help each other survive. The murders and pestilence were just part of the daily circle of life. No benefit was seen in reporting them just to rile up an already stressed population. Countries had begun to share resources openly. Sanctions were lifted and conflicts over religion, commerce or power were things of the past. Survival – the human need to survive was the rule of the day.

The launch pad was lit at night by timed infrared spotlights. The reflection gave the space capsule and rocket launchers a pinkish hue. A billowing vapor cloud exited from the base of the rocket and slowly rose to the transparent exit doors high above the capsule's cone shaped tip. These exit doors would open as soon as the ignition phase began. It was early in the morning according to Earth time. Martin moved cautiously along the transom that led to the elevator that would take him to the hatch entrance of the capsule. He had checked the list of supplies, secured his sleeping quarters and dressed in his spacesuit and helmet. He had received the results of the Apellonauts' testing of Erin as she was instilled with the stream and particles. Since it was concluded that there had been a hairline crack in Jack's helmet allowing particles to enter his respiratory system and migrate to his brain and endocrine organs, he felt more confident that Erin was okay.

The defective particles were absent from any of the streams manufactured at Maxim following the testing. Erin had been resting in her living quarters. 0-11 recorded his observations of her post-test activities and condition to SIES and the Apellonauts. She did not appear to have any side effects. In fact, she had tremendous energy, increased mental acuity and could perform many tasks efficiently at the same time. Another interesting observation was that she looked younger, her hair was shinier, and her vision had sharpened, allowing her to discern surface details from orbit without magnification.

Martin flipped the switches to begin the ignition process. He secured himself in the pilot's chair omitting attaching the monitoring leads used to send vital signs to the mainframe. The infrared lights responded to the change in the sound when the rockets prepared to launch. Inside the space station the crew slept. A red flashing light inside the capsule notified Martin that the rockets had moved on to phase II. The liquid oxygen had been compressed enough to provide power to carry the capsule through the exit hatch and into space. Martin flipped the three switches that forced the rocket chambers into ignition and blastoff—Phase III. He could feel his heart racing with excitement and the tiniest bit of regret that he was disobeying orders. With a deep roar the rocket and capsule began to rise off the launch pad. The crew awakened and drowsily tried to orient themselves to what was happening. Gerald, Wayne and Henry were sure the roar was coming from a rocket being launched. After the cobwebs cleared and they threw on some clothes they ran to the launch area just as the exit doors closed, the fiery tail of the rocket disappearing into space.

"Check Martin's bunk!" Gerald yelled. "That damn fool! I should have locked him up the moment he started itching to go." Wayne and Henry just shook their heads. They had both seen how Martin looked at Erin before she left for Apello. He most certainly had more than professional feelings for her. Martin, though, was the last scientist they would have suspected to disobey orders. He followed the rules to the letter.

"I guess love overrides obedience," Henry whispered to Wayne.

"He's gone! His quarters are locked, and his space equipment is not in the prep locker. Get on the intercom and see if he will answer! He doesn't have any of the monitors hocked up either. I guess we will have to track his flight and hope he makes it to the planet. Those two must have drank something that pulls them toward this planet and the Apellonauts." Gerald stared at the computer as it tracked the space capsule heading toward Apello's atmosphere. The rocket would detach at the edge of the atmosphere. That would be the part of the trip that would be up to Martin to navigate. He would have to navigate the capsule through any atmospheric storms or radiation belts surrounding the planet. It would take excellent piloting skills to make sure the capsule was able to navigate precisely so that it did not shoot beyond the surface and into the unknown.

Erin returned to her daily routine. She noticed her respiratory and heart rates had decreased more since the testing project. Though the requirements for oxygenation to her cells had diminished she found she was much more alert and could perform multiple tasks with ease and efficiency. It seemed her abilities had improved since the testing. The SIES robots, 0-11 and 0-12, were functioning at an increased level and their human-like organs had atrophied to the point of being difficult to visualize when scanned. Erin had not experienced any untoward effects of the particle revisions. Her reports to SIES on the space station were enthusiastic and detailed. She had been informed that Martin had commandeered a rocket and space capsule heading for Apello. She was surprised that the efficient and rule abiding man had broken quite a few rules. She smiled as she accessed the space capsule's progress as it gradually sped into Apello's atmosphere. She was able to contact Martin and guide the capsule through his descent thus avoiding several radiation storms and asteroid fallout. Martin guided the capsule to the surface of the planet close to where Erin's living and working modules were located. Erin had developed an emotion she had not experienced in her life on Earth. It was a kinship, a bond, with the Apellonauts and with Martin. The emotion was peaceful and satisfying. She wondered if Martin felt the same emotion. Martin had to use all of his strength to steer the capsule through the obstacles and to assure it landed upright. The capsule landed without any damage. Martin breathed a sigh of relief as did the SIES crew who was monitoring his journey.

"I apologize for breaking the rules and commandeering one of our spaceships. I can't explain this strong feeling that I needed to travel to Apello. I am truly sorry, but I know I can assist the Apellonauts with their projects. They gave me permission to join Dr. Coutcher and to work with them on manufacturing safe streams and particles." Martin explained tenuously. He sat for a moment with his eyes closed before unlatching his restraints and contacting Erin and the Apellonauts.

Dr. Szechnick, your next step will be to receive the gravitational apparatus through your exit port. It is being placed at this time. After applying the apparatus. you will open the exit doors and be escorted to the SIES living quarters. There you will meet with Dr. Coutcher who will brief you on the changes we are making to the particles in streams. We have returned her to her living and working area as she had no untoward reaction while observed at Maxim. The Apello voice instructed. Martin was able to interpret the communication without the direct assistance of a SIES robot. Martin was anxious to see if Erin had changed in any way since living on Apello and being subjected to the experimental development of particle changes. He knew that the breathing and circulation requirements were different on Apello for humans. He also knew that the SIES robots no longer had functioning humanoid internal organs. After application of the gravitational apparatus, he pushed the button that opened the exit door to the capsule. His eyes had to adjust to the radiant blue glow enveloping the surface structures. A giant mountain with a spongy surface towered over the three living quarters and work modules Erin had erected when she first arrived on Apello. Walking on the planet's surface was strange at first. It seemed to Martin that he would have to use very few muscles to navigate in the planet's atmosphere even with the gravitational apparatus attached. When his brain focused on the laboratory workstation he was propelled there with very little conscious use of his legs. Lifting one leg to begin walking in that direction quickly moved both legs so rapidly that Martin was at the entrance to the lab without realizing he had walked there. There was no door at what appeared to be an entrance until Martin was about six feet in front of a small indentation in the surface of the module. An opening appeared. Martin walked through it, and it closed behind him. The wall from which the opening appeared became solid again with no distinguishing marks that there had been an opening at all. The laboratory was brightly lit with some kind of lighting emitting from the walls, ceilings and floor. Erin was seated at one of a group of computers recessed into the walls. She looked up and saw Martin standing some distance from where she sat. She smiled and stood for a moment, then moved swiftly toward Martin, hugging him awkwardly.

"Martin, I am so surprised you broke rules to come to Apello before the bosses were ready to send you. This is so unlike you. Are you in trouble?" Erin asked. She looked amazing – younger and thinner. Martin wanted the hug to last, to turn into a passionate kiss but he resisted pressing against her.

"It's so good to see you, Erin. You look wonderful. I couldn't resist the pull to be here on Apello, with you and the aliens. I can't explain the alure, almost like a magnet keeps pulling me in this direction."

"I know, Martin, I feel the same bond since our first visit with the Apellonauts. I was just ordering lunch. Would you like something? The aliens are great at producing delicious earthling food. Amazing what laser and radiation technology can do. As you know, my cardio-respiratory system is very efficient. I don't require near the amount of food I needed on Earth."

"I am kind of hungry. I'll just have some soup and a sandwich if they have it." Erin turned back to one of the computers and typed in both of their requests. She motioned Martin over to the bank of computers suspended in the transparent walls.

"This is the manufacturing section of Maxim. That building is where Apellonauts are "born", produced and also where the streams are manufactured and injected with particles that eventually will perform assigned tasks. During the testing I was involved in the Apellonauts found an aberrancy in the particles when they entered the brain and endocrine systems of humans. These particles developed claws that caused them to latch on to those organs and incite changes. The Apellonauts are correcting the problem. They will need your help at Maxim in order to assure the human organs are no longer affected and also to inject emotion into the emotionless work of the aliens."

The voice of Apello interjected over the speaker system. *We see that Dr. Szechnick has arrived at the laboratory. When both you and Dr. Coutcher have finished the eating function a worker Apellonaut will take you to Maxim to work on the particle project. How long with Dr. Szechnick be staying on Apello?* Erin looked at Martin and they both telepathically communicated that they were here to stay unless they are not welcome as permanent citizens.

"*Dr. Szechnick and I desire to set up permanent residence on Apello. Our crew on the space station is also planning to make this their home. Of course, this is only if Apellonauts agree to that collaborative. We assure you that none of the crew and leaders from SIES have any desire for aggression. We wish to live peacefully and contribute to your studies of humans as much as we can.*" Erin spoke telepathically in the Apello language. 0-11 and 0-12 stood unflinchingly some distance from the two scientists. They no longer had any human organs. What had been overlooked in their development was the instillation of basic values, fair judgement and peaceful resolution of aggression as had been programmed into the aliens.

Apellonauts are interested in studying humans, especially these things called emotions. You are welcome to set up your city in the area with the present modules. There is plenty of Nitrogen and the replacement for your oxygen to support large numbers of humans for many of your Earth years. The aging of your humans will be much different from how age affects you on your planet. We will both benefit from observing each other's systems and history. Are any of your crew well versed in Earth's history?

"Thank you for your acceptance of us into your community. We have two very knowledgeable crew members that have a vast knowledge of our evolution and the development of the planets in our Earth's universe. We will communicate the invitation to join your society to our commanders and crew. We are excited to work together to share information about each other's history. Erin and Martin ate the food prepared for them hastily. They could not wait to let Gerald, Wayne, Henry and the rest of the crew know they were welcomed to establish residency on Apello. 0-10,0-11,0-12 did not understand the excitement they saw from their two crew members. They only responded to programmed orders. They had not evolved into AI models such as the Apellonauts, able to think, problem solve and react fairly to new information. The last program they received was to report unusual actions or side effects resulting from Erin's testing at Maxim. When they saw her hugging Martin and the two of them celebrating in the lab, they reported it to SIES and to the Apellonauts.

Unusual activity logged. Doctors Coutcher and Szechnick engaged in sustained physical contact. Motive unclear: possible distress or covert communication. 0-10 and 0-12 preparing rescue program. 0-10 and 0-12 began to move across the floor of the lab toward Erin and Martin. Both of the enthused astronauts had moved to the computers to plan the next missions to Apello. They would have to construct several more living quarter modules and ensure that there was enough breathable air available to fill the modules and a source to fill tanks for exploration outside of the quarters and lab. The astronauts would have to learn how to construct earth food from the planet resources and other processes.

0-10 and 0-12 grabbed Martin and Erin as they waited to receive communication from Gerald and Wayne.

"What are you doing?" Erin yelled at the robots. Martin attempted to wrestle one arm free so he could reach the control module at the back of 0-10. The robot was extremely strong.

Robots have observed unusual behavior in humans. Following command to subdue humans and to report to Apellonauts we advanced toward Erin and Martin.

"No, robots! The actions you observed are greetings! This is not activity produced from the tests at Maxim. Halt all activity at once!" Erin shouted at the robots in Apello language. She hoped that they might respond to orders from the Apellonauts. She, too, tried to reach the programming module on 0-12. 0-11 was blocking the exit door to prevent an escape. When Erin shouted the command 0-11 moved away from the door and the other two robots released their grasp on Martin and Erin. Both of them re-programmed the robots to stand near the exits and to ignore non-threatening physical contact between the two doctors. They both felt safe since over 48 hours had passed without any untoward effects from Erin's tests.

CHAPTER XII

2025

The third fleet of massive vessels, dubbed space taxis, was nearly ready to launch from several progressive nations. Each huge spacecraft was designed to accommodate two hundred people, a selection of animals, and equipment deemed necessary to inhabit Mars. An International Space Program Committee had been formed as scientists reported the dire condition of planet Earth due to its orbital position, global warming, and pollution. Several continents, including North America, had lost 20 to 30 percent of their coastline to sea-level rises of over nine feet, violent hurricanes, tornadoes, tsunamis, and earthquakes. Many states that had been inland were now located along the oceans and the lengthy high temperature seasons destroyed crops and drinking water supplies. The struggle for basic food and water led to battles and countless lost lives. The passengers on the spacecraft had been selected by government lottery to include the best scientific minds, the healthiest citizens and the potential to reproduce, ensuring the colony's future. Emily was now 75 years old in Earth years. She and Madeline had both been selected to take the journey to

Mars. Should they reach Mars and survive, Emily and Madeline would be in their sixties. All of the passengers were placed in a training program utilizing information obtained by the first SIES team before their journey to Apello. Once on Mars the passengers who were chosen to lead the various teams from Earth would attempt to communicate with Apello. Martians had long ago communicated and worked with the AIs from Apello and other planets. These advanced beings had discarded emotions in their programs as well as any aggressive tendencies and were agreeable to human migration. The study of such logically advanced beings would be both beneficial and instructive. They wanted to study the effect these emotions had on decision making in order to understand why they had been eliminated from their programming.

Emily hoped to be able to speak to Gerald. It had been so long since she had heard his voice. She received, through Madeline, reports sent via Mars to Earth from SIES members years from when they actually occurred. She had kept her journalistic column of the SIES team controlled and believable. As far as the Earth's inhabitants knowing about Apello, this was never mentioned. They were told those team members had been sent to Mars to prepare for the space taxies delivering thousands of earthlings at staggered intervals over the year of 2025. Participating countries had to sequester passengers in undisclosed locations to protect them from those desperate to survive at any cost. Scarce food and water could turn reasonable people into raving maniacs capable of killing their own children to survive. More affluent people could afford security guards and the black-market prices of food and water. The population of the Earth was shrinking as well as the inhabitable continents. Many species of wildlife, insects, fish and reptiles were extinct because of the water temperature, decrease of their usual places of inhabitance and a lack of sustenance. Some animals vital for food and resources had also been rescued and sequestered in preparation for the journey to Mars. By early 2024, the average continental temperature was 118 degrees Fahrenheit. Looting, shootings, and rioting in the cities was out of control. Even the police and other first responders became part of the chaos. Rural towns were abandoned, crops could not survive the heat or lack of water. People raided abandoned buildings, underground storage areas, even the sewers, scavenging for food and water—or hunting those they assumed were chosen for the Mars expedition. Governments crumbled unable to control the bedlam. Emily and Madeline, along with their children and grandchildren, found refuge in caves deep within the mountain ranges that still rose above the rising oceans on the newly formed west and east coasts. The people who had been selected to take this third attempt to arrive on the red planet took very few things with them. The ships had been stocked with supplies, food and water. The Earth was heating up at a much more rapid pace than predicted. Senator Eddleman was one of the few politicians scheduled for the journey. Since Richard Quincy's money had financed the building of the two prior launched rocket ships, he felt entitled to a seat on the third and final space taxi to Mars. Having been assured that Wilson Eddleman was trustworthy in this chaotic world, Quincy approached him of obtaining a reservation with Wilson. They both were in their late seventies and were not the prime participants that NASA picked to start a life on an uncharted planet with a group of superior, non-emotional aliens. Senator Eddleman had held his office for twenty-four years unchallenged. His record was unblemished. He was known for his ability to lead in a mature, rational manner regardless of the challenge. During his tenure he had engendered treaties with other countries and had strengthened the United States' position with its allies. This new world certainly would be a challenge. There were so many unknowns. Should this group of ships survive and land on Mars, they would have to engage with the Martians without disrupting the aliens' society. Would they fit in at all? Would some of the earthlings have a propensity for aggression even though the people had been scrutinized, interrogated and educated on the information they had received over the years from SIES? Decisions earthlings made based on emotion would be of little value to the Martians other than their curiosity about emotions in general.

August 22, 2025, was the date chosen to fire up the first thirty space taxies. China, The Arab countries, Mexico and the Central American countries would be the first to blast off along with the U.S. Communications had been sent to the nations that had built these Noah's Ark-like space taxis, instructing them to be ready. They were predicted to arrive on August 30, 2027, in Earth years. Martians were notified of the expected number of visitors and approximately when they should arrive. Preparation of a landing site near the mountains was planned and executed with perfect symmetry. The animals would be transported in protective bubbles to withstand the weak gravity and alien atmosphere. A special pod would be constructed and breathable air, similar to the composition Erin, Martin and the robots were using, would be pumped in from the Nitrogen rich air surrounding the planet. Work and living quarter pods would be constructed near the space taxies. A farm pod would be built for the qualified scientists to use to produce food from the material in the soil and also from the mountains. Earthlings would be taught how to use the special guns used to repair and build new construction the Apellonauts used. It seemed callous to choose participants for this final attempted exodus to Mars. The people and other inhabitants of Earth were at risk of extinction. The people chosen for this final group of expeditions were at risk of annihilation or retaliation by the Martians. Though the Martians had long ago realized the futility in aggressive acts the Earthlings were fearful because of propaganda that painted all alien beings, whether human-like or robotic, as aggressive and unfeeling enemies. The previous attempts to land on Mars had failed for several reasons. NASA had not received the additional funds to ensure the safety and durability of the spacecraft. One of the two previously launched spacecraft exploded shortly after lift-off from a defect in the cooling systems in the launch vehicle. The second and third spacecrafts had made it within ten-thousand miles from Mars atmosphere. A large meteor shower attacked the ship and knocked them far off course. With the inability to repair damage to its oxygen storage areas, the passengers and crew succumbed to oxygen deprivation. Thanks to the funds Richard Quincy provided, this last fleet of space taxies were built with fail-safe equipment, highly trained crew members who were expert in performing repairs outside and inside the ships. The people chosen to participate in the mission had been educated for several years after the failed attempts. The population of the world had diminished greatly, inadvertently slowing the damages from carbon emissions and waste production. Psychologists were included in the exiting population in order to head off mishaps that could endanger relationships with the Martians as well as with their fellow Earthlings. One Psychologist and one Psychiatrist were assigned to each space taxi to oversee and treat any mental or emotional disturbances. These professionals were also very interested in how Martians and other alien robotic beings performed without the effects of emotions. The information they received from the virgin SIES experts portrayed the aliens possessing a basic "goodness" and practical ethnicity without emotions effecting that level of mature thought. If humans could funnel their emotions into a center based on knowledge and experience rather than judgement and resentment they would live longer, avoid stress induced negativity and be much more productive. Cooperation, commitment and societal peace would result. No one wanted to become a robot, negate the ability to love, or to reduce reproduction to a computer chip's function. Were there artists, musicians, counselors and other forms in the robotic culture whose professions were fueled by emotions? Maybe none of those things were needed. What a stark, muted world that must be, thought the people who were boarding the ships on the night of August 21, 2025. Some gazed back with tears at the world they would never see again. Others dared not look, fearing they would turn and run back toward a doomed Earth.

August 22, 2025, arrived. The exodus of the participants from their sequestered hiding places took place through tunnels that had been excavated deep underground in the various lands. Those scheduled to leave in the first wave were secretly transported to the space taxi sites. Senator Eddleman and Richard Quincy were chosen to take the first taxi to blast off from the United States. Chin Ho Lin, the Esteemed Ruler of China, along with the Head of the Golden Dragon police and other dignitaries, was to leave shortly after the U.S. spacecraft launched. The Vice-President of the United States, Henry Wexler, would leave on the first taxi. The U.S. President would leave on the second wave of ships two years after the first group. Kathryn Abbott was the first black woman president in United States' history. She elected to complete her term of office and leave with the second wave. She would do her best to urge those humans left in the world to continue to attempt to decrease the destructive forces of climate change. The other countries would follow once they had received confirmation the U.S. and Chinese spacecraft had launched safely and successful separation of the space taxi from the launch rockets was accomplished. Astrophysicists had studied patterns of meteor showers and other space "junk" calculating the best time for the space taxies to enter outer space. The voyage to Mars would be long and treacherous. Each person on the huge vessels had a job to do. The psychological impact of this journey could only be soothed by convincing each traveler that they had an important part in saving mankind. Together with the Martians they hoped to establish a beneficial partnership and a community of cooperative existence. Though the planet Mars was only partly inhabitable, its size afforded more than enough space for the people from Earth chosen for the mission.

It took eighteen hours for the crew and passengers to board their space taxies and to prepare the ships for a coordinated blast off. The twelve-hour time difference between the U.S. and China had to be factored in as well as the differences of the other countries scheduled to leave in this first wave. The total time estimated to reach the atmosphere of Mars was two to two and one-half years. That is if there were no complications. There was a total of thirty ships between the countries. Five waves or missions were planned, thirty ships with each wave. Each wave would leave two years after the previous wave. There were so many factors that could change the plans. What if the world deteriorated more rapidly? What if there were huge cataclysmic disasters? What if the expertise to run the missions were not available in the years to come? What if the ships were attacked by desperate people who had not been chosen for a mission? So many possibilities. They had to take the risk and have faith that the chosen leaders would survive and could manage two hundred people per ship.

All participants other than the flight crew entered their life support capsules in the main gathering area of each space taxi. Monitoring equipment, feeding and elimination tubes were attached and the capsules closed. The rocket launchers were programmed to begin pressurizing at 8:00 AM in the States and at 8:00 PM their local time (coordinated to match the launch window). The participants had been trained for their mission. They were ready to commit to a new life, leaving the Earth behind. Though they all had been desensitized to the sorrow of leaving loved ones and their planet, some tears were shed, and heart rates climbed as the rockets' rumble vibrated through the capsules. The crews were seasoned pilots and astronauts, many having been on space missions prior to this one. The difference was that they would not be returning, and the destination had only been tested by the SIES crew five years before.

In each of the countries the Earth inhabitants that had not been chosen for the Mars missions became aware of rockets launching huge spaceships. Each country had a plan for managing the questions and anxiety that would be displayed. Many of the Asian countries' populations were accustomed to lack of information from their governments. The United States' leadership had freedom of the press that other countries lacked. The plan to release information would have to be more transparent. The Asian countries gave very little information about the mission. Despite being accustomed to this method the population began to look for ways to find out what prompted hundreds of launchings into space. Underground technical experts in the countries where information was gagged had developed contacts with the United States that could not be traced by their governments. The public was told the missions were scientific expeditions to test Mars's habitability. Journalists and newscasters questioned this information demanding to be told the real truth. Suspicion grew because of the reported number of ships leaving the States and other countries. Emily had written her final column before being sequestered. Madeline had secured a promise from Eddleman and Quincy: Emily would have a seat on the first wave. She had retired from her job one year before the 2025 mission was to depart.

The view of the Earth diminished as the rockets launched space taxies from the countries included in the first wave. Participants for the second wave were taken to underground sites in the next group of five scheduled countries. These participants would be educated and trained as the first wave participants had been with the inclusion of any additional information sent from those that had arrived on the first wave. Adjustments would be made taking into consideration this information and the status of the Earth during those two years. The rocket launchers detached and burned away from the space taxies. No technical problems had occurred during this first phase. The capsules would remain closed until the space taxies' trajectory had been verified to be in line with the projected path toward the red planet. Any diversion from the course for each ship would have to be remedied by the crew and by nearby ships. Ships from the same countries or countries sharing the same language and technical equipment were positioned near each other in space. All of the ships that had launched were able to communicate with each other. Languages were automatically changed by computer programs to the native language of that particular ship's country. Such cooperation was vital to the mission. It had taken years of negotiations between leaders of the countries, space program scientists and astronauts in order to prepare for this mission. Several countries were excluded for refusing to cooperate or for denying the severity of Earth's path to destruction.

CHAPTER XIII

ARRIVAL

After two years and three months, the remaining taxis of the first exodus entered the atmosphere of their new home. Mars was viewed by the travelers with awe and a sense of melancholy. Out of the thirty taxies twenty-four survived asteroid collisions, mechanical failures, and mutinies from desperate passengers attempting to return to Earth. Space travel into uncharted territory presented several surprises. The size and trajectory of asteroids much greater in mass and speed could not have been predicted. Some asteroids exhibited a magnetic property that pulled ships toward them despite the taxies' cloaking mechanisms and powerful booster rockets. Though Psychologists were available to calm and support emotional and mental health issues there always was the unpredictability of the human psyche that reacted in violent ways. Some of the passengers and crew became ill with an unusual form of *"wasting syndrome"* that did not respond to any of the treatments known to the physicians aboard the taxies. The information garnered from this first expedition was invaluable to the scientists and astronauts responsible for the second expedition scheduled to begin as soon as the remaining taxies from the first wave had established residency on Mars.

During the two-plus years since the first launch, Earth had suffered immensely from a global lack of cooperation with the International Space Exploration Council (ISEC). The Council had been formed during 2021 in cooperation with the Global Warming Project Scientists to attempt to rescue Earth from self-destruction and to work with each country's space program to devise a plan to relocate humans and some animals to another planet. At the rate Earth's temperature was rising, the occurrences of violent storms increasing, a devastating pandemic, and riots over food and water that killed and injured countless more. The five-hundred-year prediction for Earth's uninhabitability was revised to fifty years or less.

The Martians, along with consultation with Apellonauts and other advanced aliens, had assisted the first Earthlings in adapting to the climate of Mars and building living and working habitats. An Oversight Council was formed from politicians, physicians, scientists and other dignitaries to govern and maintain order amidst the remaining Earthlings. Erin, Emily, Martin, Wayne and Wilson were on the Council. Gerald was chosen as Facilitator. Madeline had downloaded all the information from the SIES mission onto zip drives, burying one set under the basement of the main SIES building now located on the coast in Pennsylvania. Pennsylvania became a coastal state after hurricanes and tsunamis destroyed its original coastline. The second copy of the zip drives was taken aboard the taxi to which Madeline had been assigned. Her children and grandchildren had been chosen to be occupants on the second group of space taxies to leave in late 2027 or early 2028. She and her family members would be several years younger when they arrived on Mars. She prayed they could survive Earth's collapse long enough to make the journey. She had been torn emotionally when Gerald requested she agree to leave Earth on the initial mission. He wanted to utilize her computer skills and also to save his loyal friend and her family. Emily was ecstatic over the possibility of seeing Gerald. She knew he would not be living on Mars as he was responsible for the expedition to Apello and the possibility of exploration of other planets in the galaxy. She knew she would always have to share this brilliant man with space and scientific discovery. She was content to spend her remaining years with whatever moments they could share with each other.

Many of the new visitors to Mars volunteered to be studied by the Martians. A special translation apparatus was developed for each person arriving on the planet so they could communicate in their own language and also the Martian language. The Martians focused their study on the human limbic system, the brain's emotional core. The amygdala is a structure involved in many brain functions. It is part of a system that processes "reflexive" emotions such as fear and anxiety. This structure is located below thalamus in the central part of the brain. The emotional brain (paleomammalian) development occurred early in the evolution of man. Play-based behavior is an integral part in interactions between young and adult mammals. The amygdala is the affective system responsible for judgements, discernment between good and bad, safe and threatening, and friend and foe. The thalamus is responsible for emotion processing such as fear, sadness, disgust, happiness and pleasure. All sensory input, other than olfactory (smell) information, is processed in the thalamus. The ventral tegmentum, located in the midbrain, is important in cognition, motivation, responses related to love, and sense of natural reward. The VTA, (ventral Tegmentum Apparatus) releases dopamine when stimulated. Much of the

VTA activity occurs unconsciously. Martians could study any biological component by creating a non-invasive, three-dimensional cellular duplicate that can be examined without disturbing the actual cells or components from the source. Patterns of electro-chemical tracings were extracted from the replicated brains of the human volunteers. These tracings were entered into a device that was responsible for producing the computerized "brains" of robots and the Martians. 0-10, 0-11 were chosen since they still had small vital organs other than a brain. The Martians could capture any physiologic reaction of the vital organs when the emotional center was stimulated. A computerized duplicate of these electro-physiological patterns could be synthesized and introduced into the programming of a new test group of Martians for observation to see if there was any change in any of the normally programmed activities and calculations of the subject. Each Martian had an identifier assigned when it was produced. These identifier configurations bore no relation to any Earth language. The Earthlings decided to give as many of the Martians and other aliens they encountered human names. One of the Martians identified as a "test" alien for the "emotion study" project was Kurt. Kurt's name was catalogued into the study's documents along with his Martian hieroglyphics.

One emotion was tested in each of the Martian subjects at a time. There was a control group of newly produced Martians who had no emotion added to their programs. Each of the subjects were assigned tasks to perform. The tasks ranged from simple to extremely difficult. Glitches were introduced randomly that would stop or interfere with the progress of the activity to see if the test group displayed any emotion or efficiently devised a solution to complete the task despite the interference. Kurt's reaction when asked to gather tools and equipment needed to repair faulty vehicles or apparatuses was interesting. In the midst of gathering the tools to repair a computer that had been deliberately hacked by the Martians performing the tests, Kurt was interrupted several times by an emergency call to perform another task. This jeopardized the time frame he had to complete the first task. The emotion of love had been added to Kurt's computer brain. The Martians who were in the group that were not receiving an emotion completed both tasks by speeding up efficiency and time performed. Kurt seemed confused as to which task to complete first. Did *love* affect Kurt's decision-making? Would any emotion have the same effect? Kurt completed both tasks but took more time to complete them and he also did not perform as efficiently as the Martians who did not have an emotion added. Anger, fear, lust, anxiety, joy, sorrow and aggression were added to seven Martians in the study. Similar tasks and interruptions to the ones used with Kurt. Six of the Martians exhibited the same functionality that Kurt had demonstrated. Aggression was different. That Martian, named Wilbur by the scientists working with the Martians froze when the random task was suddenly introduced into the original mix. No number of overrides or computer counter instructions could thaw Wilbur. He "froze" as soon as the interference was introduced. Wilbur was taken to the laboratory where the emotion "aggression" was removed. He returned to the tasks and completed them with the same reduced timing and efficiency displayed by the other test subjects. No matter how difficult or simple the tasks, interruptions in performing an initial task did not affect the Martians in the control group but did affect the efficiency and ability to complete tasks in the ascribed time of the test group. The next set of tests introduced a second Martian whose computer brain had an emotion added. That second Martian slowed the progress of the first test Martian when both had emotions added. If neither had E1-7 (the code number for the emotion) the efficiency doubled. If only one Martian had an emotional program, the emotionless one completed the task alone. All emotions produced the same effect except "aggression". When it was placed inside either Martians computer both the assistant without the aggression and the one with it froze. Both had to be taken to the lab to be reprogrammed or rebooted.

The prolonged collaboration on the emotion experiment had deepened the bond between Martin and Erin. Their emotions had grown into romantic feelings, which they reluctantly set aside to focus on the project. Martians could see that most of the emotions affected the efficiency and ability to stick to a schedule. Descriptions of how the emotions were displayed by humans were acted out by those that had volunteered to work on the project. The adoring glances, occasional touching and almost giddy demeanor of Martin and Erin were observed by the Martians who assigned those observations to the emotion "love". Love often led to the female human to reproduce. The Martians watched Erin closely to see if her body changed like other women earthlings. The first group of humans settled into life on Mars readily. They adapted to the slower aging process and noted increases in energy and cognitive function. Having to create an atmosphere inside their work and living modules was the most difficult part. They missed the colors, the change of seasons, the outdoors. They also missed those that had been left back on Earth. The Martians collaborated with them in their business-like manner and were always polite, prompt and exceedingly intelligent. Friendship based on mutual respect and task-oriented cooperation—devoid of deep feeling—took time to accept. The project that studied placing emotions in the computer brains of the Martians had been going on for over a year. The conclusion was that any emotion except "aggression" could affect the efficiency of the Martian robotic population. "aggression" paralyzed the Martians. Even other Martians working in close proximity on the same task became paralyzed. The Martians and aliens from other planets nearby had determined the futility of aggressive behavior, wars and traumatic confrontations hundreds of light years ago. Thus, no emotions were programmed into the "brains" of the aliens.

Emily was able to speak with Gerald remotely through a program sent from the space station circling Apello. She could see him on the monitor, and he could see her. Their conversations were a testament to human emotion—love, joy, sorrow, and excitement played across their faces. Even being interrupted by meteor storms or radiation tsunamis, the two waited patiently until their images returned or they tried to reach each other at a later time. Gerald joined meetings of the Council on Mars when he could. His life and the lives of the other astronauts and scientists that lived with him on Apello had changed dramatically. They learned to document their experiments and interaction with the Apellonauts, place them in small, durable transport capsules designed to survive the wormhole and journey back to Earth. Gerald, Richard, Wilson and the scientists hoped that when and if they reached Earth their planet could be saved by the valuable information contained in them.

By 2037, Earth had made some progress in controlling greenhouse gases, pollution, waste and climate disasters. It was not enough to alter the planet's fatal trajectory toward the sun, but it did foster a mature recognition of humanity's responsibility for the coming disaster. In a grim paradox, the survivors realized that their former battles over resources had been futile. Every person on Earth needed to do what they could to slow the ravaging of Earth's resources. They had to work together globally to preserve water, produce food and eliminate waste. What aliens had learned light years ago was finally sinking into the small percentage of humans who had survived the aggressive battles in the past. They had recovered the capsules buried under SIES and awaited the arrival of any of the space capsules sent from Apello and from Mars. On September 7, 2038, three of the space capsules landed on Earth. One landed in what remained of the Atlantic Ocean just off new coastal state of Mississippi. Two others landed in China. The distance between the United States and China had changed as the Pacific Ocean shrunk and unimaginable geological forces had drawn the west coast of America and the east coast of China to within a few hundred miles of each other. The two countries had become more cordial allies since the first space taxies left for Mars. The second group of taxies had left in 2027 as planned. Only three of the five had survived the trip and planted its human cargo on Mars. The third group of taxies were destroyed before they even left Earth in the insane battles of starving Earthlings trying to desperately get a seat on the last planned exodus from their rotting Earth. People lost all reason when they were unable to get food and water. They stormed the satellite cities where the taxies awaited their crews and passengers. As people exited the underground secure sights to board the taxies they were attacked and killed. Men, women, children, animals were all destroyed, the taxis were also destroyed. Many of the passengers and crew were killed in the onslaught. The people left on Earth were mostly elderly, with little education or technical skill. There were only a few hundred in countries across the world that could understand the information Gerald and the other taxied scientists had sent to them in the space capsules. Those that physically could began to create organic farms, water treatment plants using very different chemicals to clean the water, building wind-powered grids and forming governing bodies focused on citizen needs, not political power. Aggressive acts were forbidden and dealt with immediately when they occurred. The temperature of the Earth was now at an average of 135 degrees F. The people that were healthy enough began to upgrade the living quarters where the passengers for the taxies awaited their time to depart. Oceanic villages were constructed under what remained of the great waterways. The Earth's temperature came down several degrees but not enough to allow above the ground life to survive. There was one other suggestion from the information sent from outer space to Earth. They considered constructing a planetary version of the protective capsules used around ships and habitats on Apello and Mars. and halt its dangerous journey toward the sun. Maintaining the capsule's delicate 78% nitrogen balance would be critical for its integrity. It would be transparent, so the sky, moon, sun, and stars would remain visible. It would take several years to construct and knowledgeable scientists to oversee the construction. Earth had lost so many of its young people and experts. It seemed like the project was unreachable.

Erin, Martin and Gerald received the terrible news from Earth. They brought it to the Council on Mars and asked the Martians if they had any suggestions. The emotionless Martians offered to contact their own ships and those of the Apellonauts—still observing Earth—to land and assist with the creation of the protective capsule and above ground living quarters for Earthlings. Thus began the salvage of our planet. With the assistance of the aliens, we once feared, the remaining Earthlings were able to avoid the collision of the Earth with its sun, learned the delicate balance required for life and that aggression was ultimately useless and destructive. Earthlings retained their emotions; aliens retained their expertise, and Earth survived.

ACKNOWLEDGEMENTS

My grandson was fourteen years old when he showed me the drawings of some characters he had drawn. Unlike this grandma, he leaned toward the artistic side of his father and also my sister. Both of those family members were very talented in drawing, painting, and sculpting.

"Grandma, can you write a Science fiction book about these aliens? I really like those kinds of stories." Finn looked at me with the sweetest smile, dimples and all.

I looked at the eerie, super-muscular beings with fangs protruding from something akin to lips and snake-like appendages swirling around an oblong face with bulging eyes dangling from their orbits. It had several appendages, and each one held hatchets and ray guns. The female component wasn't too different in the looks department, other than very large mammary components bursting from her plaited chest armor. I wanted to gently query the origin of the idea for her garment, but I thought I would do better by staying away from that subject. "Honey (he hates when I call him those soupy names), I haven't ever written a science fiction book. I thought I had a pretty hairy thriller when I wrote Orphans, but I used to love going to the Planetarium in New York, and also the one at college in town. I'm not sure I could write a story as good as these aliens you have drawn." I stared at his aliens on his paper, then at him. The dimples and his downcast expression got to me. "Okay, I'll give it a try. I will have to do a lot of research. Even when I write a fictional book, it still has to have some real facts in it."

He gave me a half-hug and asked what we had to eat (this would be the fifth meal of the day). My writing stories, letters, and poems began in the second or third grade. I rarely slept more than three or four hours at night. That was true even as a baby. Perhaps I have too much adrenaline, my mother would say. There may have been other reasons mentioned in my memoir, The Tire Swing.

I developed a passion for writing, caretaking, and overdoing from my dear Mother, Ethelyn. She attended the Juilliard School of Music in New York at age fifteen and played the grand piano at Carnegie Hall at age seventeen. She wrote stories and poems that were never published. My Father, Walter, had a photographic memory, read voraciously, and was a very talented photographer. The patience and understanding of my family, my sisters, Ethel and Alice, and my husband, John, who has to listen to my edits and late-night rants, are a family of wonderful, crazy, talented, loving people. My teachers, especially Ms. Toma and Ms. Saks, both advanced literature instructors at Waite High School, taught me the magic of the written word. To Mike Ross who took my scribblings, grammar aberrations, off-the-wall plots, and misguided protagonists and taught me how to turn my dreams into tales across many genres. To my dear friends, Kitty, Linda, Karen, Robbie, Tammy, Bonnie, Lynn, and so many others who supported me, encouraged me, laughed with me, and cried with this shy girl who never thought she could do anything right and told her she was worthy – "just write!'

My life's work has unfolded at the intersection of service and compassion. I spent my career in the healthcare field, serving as a nurse, consultant, compliance officer, hospice specialist, legal nurse consultant, coding specialist, educator, and supervisor. In every role, I bore witness to the fragility and resilience of the human spirit. Beyond my profession, I have remained devoted to community service, volunteering in blood drives, community health fairs, and home-care initiatives where care is not merely given, but shared.

Writing entered my life when I was eight years old and never truly left. What began as a quiet inclination became a lifelong calling one that grew alongside experience, loss, faith, and love. Over the years, I have written hundreds of poems, crafted personal greeting cards, prepared legal and clinical narratives, authored policies, and contributed professional magazine articles. Writing became both refuge and testimony: a way to make sense of the world and to give voice to what is often left unspoken.

A defining influence in my journey as a writer came during my senior year at Waite High School, where a demanding, college-level literature teacher shaped my discipline and sharpened my voice. Her rigor taught me that words matter that clarity, honesty, and courage are essential to prose that endures.

My poetry has been published in the *National Library of Poetry*. I share my life with my husband, John, and together we are blessed with five children, fourteen grandchildren and four great-grandchildren each one a living reminder that love multiplies when it is given freely.

I am a local author whose work spans multiple genres, rooted in family, faith, service, and lived experience. Whatever the future holds, I intend to remain faithful to the work of reflection and creation, just as I have throughout my career and well into retirement.

I write because it is how I listen.

I write because it is how I remember.

And, by grace, I will keep writing.